CHERISH

TREASURE - 4

JESSA JAMES

GET A FREE BOOK!

Join my mailing list to be the first to know of new releases, free books, special prices and other author giveaways.

http://freehotcontemporary.com

1

FIORE

$\mathcal{T}$he bullet left the gun. The breath left my body. My temple throbs, a remnant from Tony's violent temper. The air around me seemed to vanish, bleeding out in a rush. My muscles lock up, freezing me in my tracks.

It feels like I am being crushed and crumpled as I stood there, staring at the two men. The whole world is stained red as I waited for one of the men to die.

One is my kidnapper turned lover. One is my brother turned enslaver. They wrestle on the ground before me, fighting over me. Their eyes are filled with hatred for one another, their grappling violent.

Whichever one I shot, I have to live with not just his death, but the life laid out for me by the survivor. I have no real options in this scenario.

They've left me none.

It's an impossible choice, yet... somehow, I blink, and I've already pulled the trigger.

My aim is true, though I tremble as I take the shot.

The loud report of the gun startles me. Monster and Tony don't even have time to react to the sound before the bullet takes the back of Tony's skull off.

There's blood everywhere, although with my red-stained vision it looks black to me. Blood sprays in all directions, especially outward from the wall where the bit of skull landed. It keeps bubbling up from where the back of his skull is missing, Tony's exposed brain pulsing and pumping out blood.

A tide of nausea overwhelms me, rising up in my throat. Tony slumps down against Monster's chest. Monster seems frozen as if he's unsure what has happened to Tony.

Suddenly, I am unlocked. I can move again.

The nausea threatens again, gagging me. I drop the gun carelessly, turning away from the scene I just caused. I try to cover my mouth to hold the vomit in my throat, but it bubbles up just like the blood from Tony's corpse.

I fall to my knees and retch violently, the vomit falling onto the pristine wood floor. I hear Monster move behind me, hear him wrestling with Tony's body.

"Shit," he mutters quietly. Then, "Are you alright?"

Retching again, I close my eyes against the whole entire world. For just a moment, I need to not be the girl that murdered her brother. The girl who is shivering and vomiting while the entire world spins around me.

Someone else tries to enter the room, but Monster gets rid of them. "Go back to your rooms. Don't come out until you're told to."

He's clearing the area of witnesses. Witnesses that

could tell everyone what I've done. I'm at once humbled and ashamed.

Though it wasn't a choice I wanted to make, a tiny voice inside says that I obviously made the right one. Monster is already proving that.

I feel his hand on my back, a gentle caress. Monster rubs my upper back for a second as I double over miserably. I just killed my only brother that stuck around. The only family member that I still had any interest in talking to.

No, I didn't kill him. I *murdered* him.

It feels surreal like I imagined the whole thing. I stare at my trembling hands dumbly. Why aren't they covered in blood, then? It feels like they should be. Did I really kill him?

But a glance behind me at Tony's crumpled body tells me that I didn't make it up. I wipe the vomit from my mouth and wince as Monster draws a blanket over Tony's body.

Monster looks at me, his expression brooding. "Come on. We need to get you out of here."

He helps me off the floor, putting his arm around my shoulders and guiding my shaky steps to the door. I grip his arm, nails digging into his flesh through his button-up shirt. I'm still crying, the only sound in the house is that of my hysterical sobs.

"Stay here for a second, Fiore," Monster orders, parking me by the front door. He tries to pry my hands from his forearm, but I burrow my face against his chest, making a low keening sound.

I *need* Monster. Need him with me. I won't let go if it

means he won't leave my sight. In this uncertain world, this world I just helped to create when I fired that shot, he's the only person I can rely on.

He seems surprised by my clinginess, his free arm coming back down to pat my shoulder. "It's okay, Fiore. It will be okay, I promise."

I squeeze my eyes closed and release a sob as he disentangles himself. He steps away through the doorway to the living room, keeping one eye on me while he pulls out his phone. His phone calls are hushed, but in the silence echoing throughout the house right now, they sound loud.

"I need you to come here, to the house," he orders. "There is a body. I need it taken care of." He pauses, listening intently. "No, I think we'll be gone. Yes. Alright."

He hangs up, casting one last glance around the living room. Monster runs his hand over the bottom half of his face. I watch the gears in his head churn for a moment.

Then he turns toward me. We make eye contact as he walks over to the front door.

"We're going to go now," he says, his Greek accent thicker than normal. "You and I will find a hotel to stay in for a bit. How does that sound?"

I nod, wiping my eyes with the back of my hand. He opens the front door, escorting me out to the curb. We only wait a moment before a sleek white SUV pulls up. Monster hustles me into the back seat, sliding in beside me.

I can feel the judgment coming off the driver as he surveys me. I must look like a complete wreck and smell like vomit.

"Take us to the Belvedere Hotel," Monster says, in that no-nonsense tone of his. He slips his arm around my shoulders and I unabashedly burrow against his chest, hiding my face from the world.

As the SUV pulls out, I'm overwhelmed by my own thoughts.

I murdered a man.

Worse, I murdered my own brother.

Tony could very well have been the last I'll ever see of the Carolla family. According to Tony, my father and brothers are dead and gone.

Supposedly, killed by the only man I have left, the man I cling to right now.

I keep picturing Tony, in the moments before I shot him. He wrestled on the floor with Monster, his face bright red with rage. There was murder in his eyes.

If I hadn't shot him, he would have killed Monster without question. And then he might have killed me too, while he was at it. There was really no telling with Tony.

The logical part of my brain says that what I did was right. But the louder, more emotional part of my brain is still devastated. I don't know what's wrong with me.

Or maybe I do know, and that's the problem. Maybe the issue is that I don't know who loves and who is just using me, who plays with my heart and who laughs when I hurt. How can I have any idea, when Monster and Tony are the only men in my life?

Monster shifts, clearing his throat. The words come almost out of nowhere, soft and quiet. "Thank you, Fiore. I know he was your brother, but... thank you."

The tone of his voice is the closest thing to remorse

I've ever heard from him. All I can do is nod, rather than letting the kaleidoscope of thoughts leave my mouth. I swallow, burrowing against him.

When we get to the hotel, Monster pulls me from the car, sweeping me off of my feet and cradling me close. I let my eyes close, shutting out the rest of the world.

Monster carries me upstairs, his arms strong and true. He carries me into a bedroom, setting me on the bed. Without a word, he starts undressing me. Shoes on the floor, dress over my head, bra and panties cast aside.

I realize I'm still crying, soundless tears falling down my cheeks. The weight of my eyelashes is so heavy right now, so I let my eyes drift to a close a final time.

He tucks me into the big bed, lying on my side facing him. He turns off the lights and then comes back to me, sitting with me. His warm fingers run through my hair as he lulls me to sleep.

My last thought is that I am very glad that he is here.

2

ARSEN

I stand by the window of the Belvedere Hotel penthouse suite, looking out at the sunrise. Well, it's not really the sunrise any longer. It's officially the morning, as the sunlight blossoms over the oak trees on St. Charles Avenue. As I watch the street below, a streetcar stops, letting people off and picking a few up.

The Belvedere penthouse is only ten stories, so I sip my coffee and look down on the people below like some kind of demigod. A few people are up and moving this way or that, crossing the street to get to their service industry jobs. Maybe coming back from late-night employment in the French Quarter, who knows.

Behind me, Fiore stirs in the bed. I turn my head and look at her, but she's still just a lump beneath the covers. I slept in the other room for a few hours, afraid almost to leave her alone for too long. She seemed more fragile than ever in the moments just after she killed Tony, desperate and lonely and insane with grief.

When I came back, I was relieved to find her still

breathing. She had tunneled under the comforter, rest-lessly tossing and turning in her sleep. So, I ordered coffee from room service and stood guard.

Keeping a watch, if you will.

I frown at the people walking down below, ruminating on the events of yesterday. I'm not sure how Fiore came to save my life, especially when she could've had her brother in my stead. How she could point a weapon at the two of us and shoot Tony, I'm not sure.

But I am grateful, after a fashion.

Who would have guessed that the girl I abducted could be the girl that saved my fucking life later? Not me, of that I am certain.

I must admit, seeing her after she pulled the trigger... watching the horror on her face when she realized the gravity of what she'd done...

There is something about killing a person, a person who's not attacking you, that just changes you forever. Watching the indelible marks of unquestionable murder sink in on Fiore's face was both painful and beautiful.

Now, she truly belongs to me in a way that she didn't before. A deep pool of emotion stirs beneath my surface, though I am careful not to let it show.

I am nothing if not a vigilant man.

Pulling out my cell phone, I text Bill, my "fixer", asking for an update. He replies almost instantly, saying that the house has been cleaned thoroughly and the body disposed of.

I release a heavy breath, setting my coffee down on the table by the window. Fiore stirs again, yawns, and uncovers her face.

Her eyes search for me. When she finds me, she looks a little surprised.

"You're here." It comes out low and breathy.

"You seem surprised," I say, walking over to the bed. I stare down at her, pinning her with my gaze.

"No. Not exactly," she says, sitting up. She pushes her fingers through her hair. "God. I need a shower."

I incline my head toward the bathroom. "It's that way. I have some new clothes for you, whenever you're ready."

She just nods, shivering a bit as she sheds the blanket. She's completely naked, bare before my eyes. She stands up. She's fucking stunning, not that I needed any reminder. Her skin is milky and pale, her breasts like two teardrops, her ass jutting out in just enough for a handful.

She doesn't shield herself from my eyes as she pads over to the bathroom, but she doesn't make eye contact either. Though I am stirred by her naked body, as I always am, I don't say anything.

I just let her go, knowing that she has plenty on her mind after last night. Besides, there is plenty of time for frolicking.

I realize that in the back of my mind, I no longer think that Fiore has to die to serve my purposes. I think that Katherine Carolla died some time ago. And I rebuilt her remains into Fiore, this fiery little bitch. A girl who knows my predilections, who understands my wants and needs. She has proven herself, time and again.

She's done everything I've wanted, and yet... it still isn't enough. Perhaps if she wore something that would tell everyone who saw her that she was *mine*... I think of the collar that I brought for her, a simple and elegant white gold band.

If she wears it, will that be enough?

I hear a loud sound come from the bathroom. Something shatters, and I hear Fiore curse. Striding over to the door, I open it to find Fiore sitting on the edge of the bathtub, a piece of porcelain broken into a million pieces at her feet. Behind her, the bathtub is filled with gently steaming water.

She's in tears and bleeding all over the place from cuts in her palms and fingers as she tries to pick up the pieces.

"Stop," I tell her with a sigh. I start rolling up my sleeves, preparing to deal the mess. To my surprise and consternation, Fiore jerks her head side to side, picking up more tiny pieces of porcelain.

She doesn't even seem to be aware of the fact that she is bleeding, little red rivulets leaking from her hands to land in perfect droplets on the white tile floor.

"Leave it!" I order her, scowling. My shoes crunch against the porcelain. "Put the pieces down and get in the bathtub."

Fiore looks up at me, rage written all over her features. "You don't tell me what to do."

My brows lift. "That's the basis of our relationship. I tell you what to do, you squirm. I force you to do it, you love being forced."

She throws the bloody mess she's holding at me, hitting me square in the chest with a thud. A big bloodied stain starts to spread across my crisp white button up, right over my heart. The pieces of porcelain fall to the floor. I look up, enraged.

"What the fuck did you do that for?" I sneer, moving over to her in an instant. Towering over her, I grab her by the shoulders and give her a shake, thinking that I can shake some sense back into her.

"Are you going to kill me, then?" she asks, biting off her words. "Are you going to get rid of me like you did my whole family?"

My eyes narrow at that. "Are you saying that you aren't glad to be free of them? Or maybe you liked being a piece of property?"

I push her down into the bathtub roughly. She falls in, the water splashing against her body. Still, she looks at me through slitted eyes.

"Just say it," she hisses. "Just tell me that you had my brothers and my father killed."

"Oh, little flower." My lips tip up in a smile. "I didn't have them killed. I killed them myself."

Her eyes go wide, the breath leaves her in a *whoof*. Her voice is shaky now. "No."

I perch on the end on the bathtub, by her feet. "I did. And I'm not sorry about it, not even one bit. I'm not sorry that Tony is dead, either. I'm only sad that you took his life instead of me."

Tears overtake her. "Why?"

I look down the bridge of my nose at her. "You know why. Your family was a parasite, a leech, living off the blood of others. I did the world a favor, taking all of you out. And I did you a favor, although I didn't plan it that way."

She takes a big breath. Tearstained, her breasts just peeking out of the water, she is quite lovely. "You planned to hurt me. Kill me. You said as much yourself."

"Yes." I cock my head. "I did."

"And now?" she asks, her voice gone soft and breathy.

Rather than answer, I put my hand in the water, testing the temperature. It's hot, but not unbearably so. My hand dips lower, caressing her ankle lazily. "I did kill Katherine. I killed all the Carollas. Now you're Fiore. You're my creature. Understand?"

I make eye contact with her on the last word, finding those baby blue eyes looking back at me. Somehow, those eyes are still full of innocence. They haven't been corrupted in the time that she's been with me.

I lean closer and grip her knee. She bites her lip and slowly nods. "Yes."

Sliding closer on the rim of the tub, I move my hand up her silky thigh. "I saved you. When I bought you, you became mine. My possession, my plaything. And you were forever out of their reach."

I cock my head as I brush my fingertips against her core, teasing her lips. She gasps soundlessly, her lips parting as she writhes against my invasion. My fingertips find her clit, and she let out a breathy little moan, closing her eyes.

"Look at me," I order.

Her eyes open again. I lean down and slide my fingers into her pussy. I smile wickedly.

"Tell me who you belong to," I whisper. "So that there won't ever be any doubt."

Her perfect pink lips form the words I need to hear. "You. I belong to you, Monster."

Withdrawing my hand from her pussy and from the water, I stand. "Good. I'll be waiting in the bedroom for you when you're finished. And don't cut your feet on the porcelain on your way out of the bathroom."

I leave the bathroom, already unbuttoning my bloodied shirt. The words she spoke echo through my head.

I belong to you, Monster.

But even as I begin to strip off my clothes, I know that's not enough.

When will she ever be able to quell this unease deep inside me?

3

FIORE

*T*he collar is made of white gold, finely wrought and expensive. I turn it over, considering it as I sip my coffee at the little French patisserie next door to the hotel. It's been a few days since I killed Tony, a few days of tossing and turning all night in my hotel room bed.

This morning, I got up to find Monster gone. No note, no direction for how I should spend my day.

There was only this collar on the pillow beside mine, shiny and cold to the touch.

I've seen the collar before. I know it's from him.

A gift.

A reminder.

Something that says I am his possession, without a shadow of a doubt. I'm not sure who Monster feels needs to be warned off. Is it everyone who sees me? One person in particular? Or maybe it's me that Monster can't seem to trust.

After all, we have a rocky history. We've both made mistakes that make it hard to trust each other.

I have trouble trusting myself and my feelings around Monster, honestly.

How can I trust myself, after what I did to Tony?

I murdered him. I took his life away, and for what? Because he was a jerk?

I try not to look at my palms, which are still sticky with imagined blood after the shooting. I know it's very Lady Macbeth of me, but I can't help but imagine my brother's blood on my hands no matter how many times I wash them.

It won't go away.

Nor will the fact of my life, my horrible pathetic little life as Katherine Carolla. It almost makes me glad that Monster says I died and came back as Fiore.

First, I let Tony and my brothers jerk me around like a puppy on a chain for basically my whole life. Then, I let my father set any rules he wanted for me, which only served to isolate me. Finally, my eyes were opened in the worst way possible, by a person that I myself nicknamed Monster.

So now, for me to have these... these *feelings* for him... feelings that make my stomach flutter every time he's around... Yeah, not reliable. Not at all.

I consider that as I set the collar down on the table beside me, picking up my coffee cup instead. I drain the last drops, wishing there was just a little bit more.

Isn't that always the case?

I look up and catch the reflection of a man in a mirror

before me. Tall, dark, and wearing a button up and slacks, for a moment I think that it's Monster that I see. He's approaching me, which makes my two bodyguards draw closer. I can see familiarity on the guard's faces, though.

As he gets closer, I can see a few differences between this man and Monster. Where Monster mostly wears a day's worth of scruff, this man has more of a beard. His laugh lines and crows' feet are more pronounced, but only a little.

What really sets them apart is the eyes, though. Where Monster's gaze is a chilling grey, this man's eyes have the lightest tinge of hazel. I try to figure out if his eyes are more green or more light brown, but I can't.

Stopping just before my bodyguards start to get their hackles up, he smiles at me in the mirror. That smile is all too familiar to me; it's the same grin that Monster used to wear when I first met him.

The one that used to make chills break out along my arms.

The one that said its wearer would eat me alive if I turned my back for a second.

"You must be Katherine," he says, his deep voice inflected with a melodious swirl of Greek and British accents. Just like Monster.

They can only be brothers. And since I have met Damen, this can only be Dryas.

I turn in my chair, raising a brow. "You must be Dryas, I presume."

His smile widens. "Right you are. I must say, my brother doesn't usually like his women with brains, but I can see that you are different."

My lips thin at the mention of Monster's other women. I feel a surge of jealousy, but I don't let it show.

"You look very much like him," I say.

"Yes, but better looking, obviously." He makes the statement with no trace of humor, so I can't tell if he's kidding or not. He regards me for a moment. "You aren't Arsen's usual type... but you are quite stunning."

I force my lips into a semblance of a smile. Glancing at my bodyguards, I incline my head a fraction. They step back, allowing Dryas to approach. He comes around the little table, pulling up a seat and sitting down.

His eyes glint as he settles in. "On second glance, I see what he sees in you. You look like a girl he had for a while. That was here, in this city, I think."

I soak up that information, but I'm still uncertain of his intentions. I don't trust him further than I could throw him, and with those broad shoulders and big feet, he's almost twice my size.

"Why are you here, Dryas?" I keep my tone light, pretending to pick a speck of lint off of my yellow silk dress.

"In New Orleans? I think that should be obvious. I had to meet you, Katherine."

I smile ruefully, skirting the topic of my name. "There must be a reason you are here, talking to me by yourself. I'm certain that your brother wouldn't like you approaching me alone."

Dryas looks at me for a second, his lips quirking. Then he looks around the shop. "Who do I have to murder to get a cup of coffee around here?"

"It's counter service," I say.

He hops up, heading to the counter. He fishes a couple of bills out of his wallet, dropping them in front of the wide-eyed barista.

"Coffee," he commands the young girl. "One for me, one for my companion."

Then he turns his back and returns to the table. "Problem solved."

He sits down, drumming his fingers on the wood tabletop that stretches between us. He casts an eye over my body, making me uncomfortable. I squirm just a little, and from his smile, I can see that he got the reaction he was looking for.

"How much?" Dryas asks, sliding his chair closer. He reaches out, grasping my wrist, and pins me with a hard stare. "What, do you charge by the hour? Or is it more of a week by week basis?"

I try to tug my wrist back. His grip turns painful. One of the bodyguards moves in, but I stop him with a glance.

"I'm not sure what kind of ladies you spend time with, but I assure you that I am not for sale." Even as I say it, though, my heart sinks. I'm not for sale at the moment, but that is how Monster acquired me in the first place.

And there's nothing saying that I won't be on the auction block again when Monster tires of me... assuming he doesn't just kill me outright himself. I shudder delicately, which seems to please Dryas.

"I'll take that to mean you are open to the idea, then."

I can't help my frustrated frown. "What idea?"

He pulls me closer, putting my hand on the bulge in his slacks. He's hard, which is especially distasteful to me.

"The idea of you coming to spend a little time with me, darling."

I'm so shocked by his behavior, I don't even know how to respond. This time when the bodyguards come to swoop in and part us, I don't make a fuss. I let one pull me to safety, but my rage starts to build.

"I would never do that to him," I swear, my voice shaking with anger. "*Never*."

Dryas grins as a bodyguard paws at him. "That sounds like a challenge."

"What is wrong with you?" I hiss.

He looks at the bodyguard that's in his face. "I swear, if you touch me again, I'll gut you. I'm trying to have a nice conversation with Katherine here."

"Stay back," the bodyguard orders him placidly. "Jack, take her out of here."

I'm only too ready to leave. As I turn toward the door, Dryas's voice floats to me from the back of the cafe. "I'm not even interested in you, Katherine. I'm interested in taking everything my brother has. You're just the first step."

What? Why?

I turn my head, I try to stop. But the bodyguard keeps pulling me out the door.

"Stop!" I insist. "Seriously, let me go!"

The bodyguard's movements slow. I turn back toward Dryas, scowling. "I thought you were supposed to be working together."

"Says who?" Dryas says casually, shaking off his body-guard's touch. "I'm the superior brother. You'll see that. If you come to me willingly, I'll treat you better than he does. Buy you better things, take you better places. I'll even make you my wife if that's what you want."

I try to keep my tone firm. "I already told you, I'm not interested."

Dryas smiles lightly. "Well, then you'll have to forgive me, but I will do whatever I have to do to get you. And once I have you, you'll regret making me work for it. You see, I think my brother is very fond of his little slave. And I can't just let him be happy, can I?"

"So, this is about him, then. Not about me at all." I fold my arms across my chest.

"If I gave you any other impression, I would be lying." He looks about as smug as can be. I find my fingers itching with the desire to slap that look off his face, but I would never act on it. "But I would never put you in the position of choosing between my life or your brother's. Think about that."

With that, my bodyguard drags me out of the cafe, hustling me towards a car. I get in and the car takes off, but I look back with a scowl to see Dryas watching from just outside the cafe.

He smiles that smug grin again. I whip my head around and will the car to move faster.

But his words still ring in my ears.

I would never put you in that position. Think about that.

Against my own wishes, I can't do anything else.

4

ARSEN

*I*t's the middle of the night, but I'm not asleep. I should be. I want to be. But I lie in my bed and stare at the street light stealing into my windows, look at the shadows cast on the wall by my blinds. It's been a few days since we returned to the house.

I lost my taste for hotels when I woke to my eggs cooked incorrectly for the fourth time in a row. Driven mostly by my own need to be comfortable, I pushed Fiore into agreeing that we should return.

When I followed her into the house, into the living room... she pressed her knuckles against her lips, her face screwing up in pain as she looked at the spot where her brother died.

Her reaction was heartbreaking. I found myself thinking that I pushed too soon. But before I could attempt to comfort her, she fled upstairs to her room.

Now it's been three days and three nights, and I haven't seen Fiore step foot outside her bedroom. I was worried... now I'm thinking that I might have broken her, just to be more comfortable and eat a little better.

Fuck.

The worst part is being conscious of the fact that I care at all in the first place.

I don't want to care.

I don't want to imagine her crying, imagine her in pain.

I definitely don't want to be lying awake right now, wondering if I should go to her.

What can I possibly say that will make her feel better?

What can I do to make myself not feel this... this strange twisting feeling in my gut every time I picture her reaction to seeing the living room? The fact that something that I did made her cry... and the fact that I care...

It's humiliating, and it infuriates me.

I roll over, staring at the doorway. It's dark of course, but the door is open a hair. In case Fiore calls for me in the middle of the night. I can admit that much to myself.

Closing my eyes, I sigh. I swear, I'm losing my fucking cool over this girl. What the fuck? Who am I?

Because Arsen Aetós would not be lying in his bed, moping about some girl.

"Monster?"

Fiore whispers my name, so softly I think I might be imagining it. I open my eyes and look over to find her standing in nothing but an old t-shirt, eyes rimmed with red. Sitting up, I pretend that I wasn't just thinking about her.

"Fiore," I say. I draw back the blankets on my bed, indicating that she should come in.

She hesitates, looking at me with a haunted expression. I would give anything to know what is going on in her head just now.

"Come here." My order is softly spoken, but my words are underlined with steel.

Fiore stumbles forward, pulled through the doorway by my command. Though there is still uncertainty and even anger in her eyes, she slips beneath the covers. She shivers a little and I pull her into my warm embrace, not minding her stiffness.

She gives a watery sigh as if she's not sure why she came here to me. I fold her against my body, molding her to my chest and my hip, making her lay her head down on me.

Fiore sighs again, her body beginning to relax. I stroke her hair, soothing her into submitting to my will. We lie like that for a while, with her just staring angrily off into the distance.

I'm trying not to wonder what's on her mind. I'm not a girl. I won't ask.

At length, she speaks, her voice still full of unshed tears. "I am so fucking angry at you right now."

I pause my idle stroking of her hair. "Why?"

She makes an exasperated sound, pushing her face against my chest as if she could disappear there. "Everything."

I smother a chuckle. This really isn't funny, it was just not the response I expected. "Can you expand on that?"

She just burrows deep down into the comforter. "We're in a world of your making. You realize that, right?"

I do realize that. It's more my world than she even

knows, but that's neither here nor there. She wants to vent; she can vent. I don't say anything, which leads her to continue on after a moment.

"You brought me to Columbia. You killed my family, which we haven't really even fully talked about, although this isn't the time. You isolated me, stripped me down, broke me, and reshaped me into this... this *person*." Her voice wobbles, growing breathy. "Then you put me in a life or death situation and made me choose. You forced me to choose you. You see that, don't you?"

I feel her tears as they fall on my chest. Bringing my arm up around her waist, I pull her against my body tightly.

Don't cry. I can't stand to see you cry.

I think the words, but I don't say them. Shifting my weight, I nuzzle her neck, the long curtain of her hair sliding against my face. After a moment, she brushes her hair back and seeks my lips with her own.

Her eyes are mostly closed, tears still hanging from her eyelashes. Her mouth is soft and warm where she presses her lips to mine.

Hungry. Entreating.

I control the kiss without thought. It's second nature. Cupping her jaw, I open my mouth to hers. Her small tongue dances with mine, her desperation growing with each moment. There is no sound in the room except for the noise that our lips make, and the soft sighs that occasionally slip from her throat.

She breaks away, sitting up and pulling the t-shirt up over her head. She's left completely naked. The idea that she is nude, mentally as well as physically. She's utterly defenseless against me, and that in itself is very exciting.

I'm wearing my boxer briefs still, but I strip those off and pull Fiore on top of my body. I'm reminded again how small she is, how I could crush her skull with little effort, snap her spine.

But I don't. Instead, I kiss her as she straddles me, groaning when she pushes the blanket away and puts her hand on my cock, guiding me to her entrance. She's already wet for me, her body begging for me without her saying a word.

I lock lips with her as my cock begins to slide deep inside her pussy. My hands are in her hair, tightening their hold as the unbelievably sweet pressure of her pussy grips my cock.

"Fuck," I breathe out. "Your pussy is so fucking wet for me."

I meet her eyes, staring intently as I set a slow rhythm. She ignores me, pushing my chest down. Sitting up, she sets her own pace, bobbing up and down on my cock briskly. She pulls out all the stops, so that her hips smash into mine, again and again, her tits bouncing every time she hits my body.

Fuck it. I stretch out and enjoy the hate-fucking for a minute. From her expression, that is precisely what's happening. She digs her fingernails into my neck, gyrating hard. I can see a sheen start to form on her face and body, droplets of her sweat.

I've never seen her like this, but it's fucking hot. I grab her ass and buck up into her, riding according to her rhythms. She throws her head back and closes her eyes.

I slip my hand down between us, using the pad of my thumb to stimulate her clit. She moans, leaning into my hand and going faster.

"Oh," she whispers, her hips moving quickly. "God, yes... oh, yes..."

She's going to come, I can see it in her face. I let go of the tight control I've been holding, pounding into her as she slams down onto me over and over.

She goes rigid for a second as her orgasm ripples through her body, making her core clench around me. I groan, not missing a beat. Grabbing her ass with both hands, I slam myself home a few more times until I can feel the orgasm bearing down on me. I come with a roar, the cum bursting from my balls and spilling inside her pussy in great gushing spurts.

For a second there, I feel like an empty shell, like Fiore milked me dry. I'm content with that, the emptiness. Fiore is still on top of me, so I reach up and stroke her back, burying my face in her breasts.

At length, she sighs and moves to lie beside me, breaking the spell. As we lie there, catching our breath and soothing our racing hearts, she's the first to speak. She doesn't look at me, she turns her face away.

"Your brother came to visit me." Her voice is distant.

"Damen?" I ask, furrowing my brow. I turn onto my side and rest my head on my arm.

"No. Dryas." She turns her head toward me. "He was very threatening toward me. I'm surprised the body-guards didn't tell you."

"Threatening?" I repeat, a bit puzzled. "He probably didn't mean what you think he meant."

"He asked what I charged by the hour," she says evenly. "And then he told me that whatever you're paying me, he could pay me more."

I let out a huff of laughter. "That's just Dryas being himself. He's an ass. We've always been a bit competitive."

"He told me he can't just let you be happy!" she says, pushing herself up. "I'm telling you, he was threatening me."

"I am sure that you felt that way, but I assure you, you're not in any danger from him."

Fiore throws back the blankets and gets out of bed, her mouth twisting angrily. She searches for her t-shirt, pulling it on over her head.

"Fiore."

She ignores me, heading for the door.

Don't leave. Stay with me.

I think the words, but again I don't say them. Without so much as a glance back, she leaves my room.

I flop back on my bed, thinking about what she said. She said that Dryas threatened her. That can't be right, can it? Dryas is a little heavy handed at times, but I'm sure he didn't mean whatever he said.

I'll have to call him and tell him not to talk to her without me present. I don't want what happened with Damen happening again with Dryas. Of course, it wouldn't be an issue if I could just get her to wear the damned collar.

It would mark her as being *mine*, as much as a ring would. Maybe more.

My eyes travel to the doorway that she just went through. It doesn't escape me that she came to me in her time of sorrow. Nor does the fact that she initiated sex with me, looking for a way to end her distress.

I'm more than okay with being her release. If anything, I'm flattered by it. It means something, her seeking me out.

I sigh and turn onto my other side, to contemplate the wall once more.

5

FIORE

I'm sitting in the kitchen, drinking a mug of green tea, and staring out the window. It's been raining for two days straight, which is not unusual weather here in Louisiana. It's just stopped about an hour ago and now I get to watch the sun peek from behind the clouds.

I startle for some reason when Monster comes in, peering down his nose at me.

"I'm going away for a couple of days," he says, coming up to me on my stool. He towers over me, reminding me exactly why I feel safe in his presence.

I shudder, thinking of how his absence will affect me. I'll be lonely. I'll be vulnerable. I set down my mug of tea with a silent sigh. I know that I will miss Monster, despite myself. But I don't put that feeling into words.

It's just too complicated for that.

He cups my jaw, tilting my face up. Our eyes meet, steel gray and baby blue. He brushes his thumb back and forth against my face, making me swallow thickly.

"I talked to Dryas," he says. "He apologizes for being intimidating. He wants to take you out riding while I'm gone, as an apology."

My brows arch dramatically. I can't believe that Monster is being so lassez-faire about his brother! "What?"

"He asked what you like. I gave him a list of things. He picked riding."

I frown, pulling my face from his grip. "You can't be serious. I don't want to see him when I'm not with you."

Satisfaction flares in his eyes, but he shakes his head. "I'm telling you, he means you no harm. Besides, the bodyguards will be with you the whole time. Nothing bad is going to happen to you."

His determination makes me wonder if I might be wrong. Maybe Dryas wasn't threatening me when he asked how much I cost?

But I'm hard pressed to find another meaning.

Monster sees me thinking and smiles. "See? You're not even sure yourself. You'll have fun, I'm sure of it."

He leans over and kisses my forehead. The action in itself is shocking.

"I'll see you when I get back." And then he's gone, leaving me in the kitchen with my rapidly cooling tea. I sigh and move to put the mug in the sink.

I have a bad feeling about Dryas, a distrust in my gut. But what am I supposed to do? Monster, my only protector, has assured me that Dryas is perfectly safe.

So, I go about my normal routine for the next few hours, until my bodyguard Jack knocks on my open bedroom door. I glance up.

"Yes?"

"Mr. Aetós has given instructions that you are supposed to meet him in Houma. We are supposed to get you to the stables out there in an hour."

"Arsen said that?" I ask, wrinkling my nose.

"No, Dryas did, ma'am. I just want you to know now because we'll have to leave soon in order to make it on time."

A frown creases my face. "Thank you, Jack."

"Ma'am," he says, inclining his head. He turns on his heel and disappears down the hallway. I'm left to change, I suppose.

Mr. Aetós indeed.

Getting out of my comfortable black cotton dress, I change into a white button up, tan jodhpurs, and knee-high black leather riding boots. I put my hair in a tight bun as if that alone will make Dryas less menacing somehow.

Grabbing a lightweight grey anorak on the way out the door, I slide into the back seat of the waiting black Mercedes-Benz.

It's an uneventful drive out to Houma. I stare out the window as we drive over raised highways, looking out over the marshy wetlands below. All that untamed wild-ness, right next to the highway bustling with cars. Rolling down my window, I sniff the salty air.

It's calming, for some reason. Really nostalgic and comforting. It lets me know I'm in Louisiana. We start to pass some sugarcane fields, the green-topped yellow cane plants towering ten feet high. Soon the cane rises high on both sides of the highway, farms making up

most of this no man's land between New Orleans and
Houma.

Peering out the front windshield, I know just where
we are going. I've been to these stables many times over
the years, for riding competitions and events.

The sugarcane fields stop, giving way to sparse
utility buildings and a few houses. We eventually pull
into the stables, a grand building surrounded by a few
outbuildings. All told, the property that the stables sit
on is probably a few acres, including a large training
ring and several trails that twist back across the whole
property.

"Jack?" I say to my bodyguard. When he turns his
head to look at me, I tell him, "Under no circumstances
are you to leave me alone with Dryas."

Jack just nods and returns to scanning the road
ahead.

When I finally slide from the car, Dryas is waiting for
me in front of the stables with a little smirk on his face.
"You came."

"I wasn't really given another option," I say coolly,
surveying Dryas. He's fully outfitted for riding, with black
jodhpurs and a white button-up shirt. He's massive, just
like his brothers are.

He sees me looking and smiles. "You want to see if I'm
as good as I look? I assure you, I'm at least as well-
endowed as Arsen."

I make a face. "No, thank you."

"The offer will remain on the table," he says with a
casual shrug. "Should we go get our horses, then?"

I roll my eyes, which only makes him smile. He starts

walking without a word from me, leaving me to trail behind him. *Why am I here, again?*

Monster may trust his brother, but I do not.

Dryas leads me into the stables, where two chestnut horses wait patiently, their leads tied to the mounting post.

"I took the liberty of picking out a horse for you," he says, gesturing to one of the horses. "I picked Belle for you. And this is Beast. They're siblings, I think."

Ignoring how presumptuous it is to pick someone else's mount, I go up to Belle. I hold out my hand, palm flat up, and let her nibble at it. "Hey, girl."

I stroke her muzzle and forelock, and she nickers gently. Glancing over to see how Dryas is faring, I see him petting Beast's great shoulder.

"Ready to go?" he says, raising an eyebrow. For a moment, his expression is so much like Monster's that I suck in a breath.

"Yes," I nod. I take the reins off the mounting post, then climb up onto the horse.

Dryas swings his leg over his mount with surprising efficiency; I'm starting to think he's done this before.

"What about my bodyguards?" I say, jerking my head toward where they stand by the wall.

"Don't worry. You'll be extremely safe with me." Dryas grins, his teeth perfectly white. "No one will dare to touch you."

I glance back at my guards. I'm not worried about other people touching me, not other people then Dryas anyway.

"I would feel better if one of them came along."

But my protest is swatted aside like so much noise.

"Don't be ridiculous. We'll only be gone an hour at the most." He grabs his reins and starts to lead me out of the stables.

Once we are out of the stables and clear of the outbuildings, Dryas picks one of the clearly marked trails. It seems ordinary enough, heading over the flat, marshy ground. In the distance, I can see that it cuts through one of the cane fields. He heads down the trail without any input from me, leaving me to follow, frowning.

This is such a bad idea. I know it, but I try to push that thought into the background as I follow Dryas.

For a while, we are both silent, looking at the wild wetlands around us. The landscape is at once bleak and teeming with life, the marsh grasses hiding a multitude of life. Frogs make their throaty calls here and there. A heron watches us as it goes about its business, picking through the water for food. Dragonflies buzz and flit from place to place, passing right in front of my nose at one point.

Dryas slides a look at me. "How are you liking that big old house? You moved in pretty recently, right?"

"I like it," I say, shrugging my shoulders. Even if I had complaints, now is not the time to air them. Not when I don't know what Dryas would do with the information.

"Mm. And how do you find living with my brother? After all, you didn't have the best start, from my under-standing."

I eye him. "I find it fine."

"Was that painful for you? Being separated from your family like that has to be traumatic."

"Of course." My lips thin and I look away.

"I heard about your little escape attempt in Columbia." He looks amused. "Unsurprisingly, it didn't go well."

I suck in a breath, not responding to that. Dryas changes the topic with ease.

"What do you think is next for you and my brother?" he asks, his mouth quirking down. "Assuming you conquer New Orleans like he plans to do, what then?"

I narrow my eyes. "I hadn't really considered that. I don't think it's up to me."

His brows lift slightly. "No? Maybe it seems that way from where you're sitting, but you really have captivated Arsen. It's amusing, seeing how much you affect him."

"Me?" I say, scrunching my brow down. "I don't think so."

"Why would I lie??" he fires back mildly.

I give him a cross look. "I'm not sure, but I have no doubt that you would."

He laughs, the sound sending chills down my spine. "You're right about that. I would lie in a heartbeat. But I don't need to, in this case. Arsen is completely infatuated with you. It's plain as day. I suppose you didn't have the luck of knowing him before you came... but I'd be willing to bet he wasn't exactly pleasant your first few days."

I blanch, thinking of waking up in that room in Columbia, handcuffed to the bed. When Arsen did show eventually, he seemed nearly insane.

I thought I was going to die, plain and simple.

Dryas guesses my expression a bit too handily. "That's what I thought."

"I didn't say anything," I retort. But we both know that I didn't need to.

"And now? I bet you aren't making that face about seeing him later are you?" He looks smug. "He's gone soft, all because of you."

I lift a shoulder, giving Dryas a Gallic shrug. "I have no claim on him. We've never talked about it."

A little pressure from my heels tells my horse that we should go faster. We start to move a little faster toward the tall sugarcane.

"No, I'm sure that Arsen has other ways of communicating things with you. Probably buried to the hilt in that sweet little pussy of yours."

"Ugh," I cry, pulling a face. "I'm going to turn back now."

Dryas's face changes instantly, like a clear blue sky all at once beset by thick, black thunderclouds. "I'm not done talking to you."

I grit my teeth, turning my horse around. I can see his muscles jump; he nearly reaches out for my reins, to make me stay.

But he thinks better of it at the last second, letting me ride off back toward the stables alone.

I'm not sure what to make of Dryas now, but one thing is for sure. I don't trust him a bit more than I did before today, that's for sure.

6

FIORE

*T*hough I don't want it to, Dryas's question lingers in my mind. What do I see for future?

I have a future if I want it. And according to Dryas, I have some say in how that future plays out. It's almost enough to make my head spin.

All through the rest of that day and the next, I keep turning that fact and that question over and over again in my mind.

Could Dryas be right? Do I unknowingly have some kind of sway over Monster? Has he really developed a soft spot for me?

Or is Dryas lying, using his words to make me think one thing when in fact it is another entirely? I'm obviously more inclined to think he's being untruthful.

But like he said, why would he lie? Of course, there is an ocean of things I can't see about what motivates Dryas. I lie on the couch, a copy of *The Odyssey* open before me, trying to figure that one out.

It's impossible, of course. I've only just started to just

get to the heart of Monster; his brothers are both mysteries to me.

My mind comes back to that question of the future though. Like a broken record, that's the only song my brain will play.

So, I go along with it. With Dryas's insistence that Monster is infatuated with me. Mostly as an exercise, more than anything.

I try to imagine the future. Monster as the doting husband, hurrying to return home to me, the darling housewife. What would we do? Would we stay here, in the Audubon Park house?

Would our relationship stay just as it is, or would it grow into something more?

God, would we eventually be one of those lovey-dovey couples with three perfect kids and a white picket fence? As much as I don't believe it, I had something not too far from that in mind before I was kidnapped.

I imagine, just for a moment, that we would be those people. Yet we would still somehow sneak off for romantic weekends in Paris and sun-filled retreats in Crete.

There would always be room for romance with us, just as there was no question that he was the more dominant one of us.

I sigh. I know it's just a daydream, but it is an awfully nice one. I try to go back to reading about Odysseus and the Sirens, but I'm not really paying attention.

By the time Monster comes back from his trip, I'm completely wound up and twisted in knots that I can't untangle. He looks dapper as always in his neatly pressed dark button-up and black slacks. Then he leans over and whispers, "Fuck, I missed you..."

I shiver and invite him to come closer. His lips find a pulse point at my neck, his big body coming down on top of mine, a heavyweight. My breath stops when he grinds his cock against my pubic bone.

Ohh. Yes, I had almost forgotten how delicious every single touch could be. Addictive, almost.

Monster's lips touch my collarbone, trailing down to my breast. I gasp and arch into his kisses, making him chuckle.

"You missed me," he says, pulling back. His expression is amused, but his grey eyes are hungry.

"Maybe," I tease.

He kisses me, making me lose my breath as his tongue slides against mine. Then he pulls away again, standing up fully.

"Behave," he orders. "I just walked in. Let me go wash up first." He pauses, then a slow smile spreads across his face. "I want you, naked and in my bed before I'm out of the shower. I hope you don't have anything planned because I'm going to fuck you so hard that you won't be able to walk straight tomorrow."

My cheeks turn scarlet as my eyes widen. With that, he turns and bounds up the stairs. I can hear him as he goes, taking the stairs two at a time.

It feels more naughty than usual, being left to prepare myself for him. For the specific purpose of readying myself for his needs. I climb the stairs slowly, heading into his bedroom and stripping down to nothing.

I lie on his bed, arranging and rearranging myself,

trying to figure out which way to present myself to him. But I can't keep my thoughts from earlier from popping into my head...

What will the future look like?

When Monster steps out of his bathroom, rubbing himself with a towel, he should be the only thing I can concentrate on. He ambles over to me, his eyes still ravenous, and he drops the towel on the floor.

I look at him, six and a half feet of perfect olive skin and well-toned muscle. He's all arms and abs, pecs and muscular thighs. And his face, with those angular cheekbones, icy grey eyes, and his dark eyebrows.

Not to mention, he has the nicest cock. I don't have much to compare it to, but when he fills me up with his cock, I almost implode every single time.

All in all, the perfect package. He comes over to the bed, grabbing me by the ankle and pulling me to the edge of the bed. But that doesn't shut me up. As he nuzzles my neck, the question bubbles up to my lips.

"What do you see for us, for the future?" I ask.

He freezes. "What did you just ask me?"

I pull my lip between my teeth, my brow dropping. "I just... I want to know where we're going. Like, *us*."

I gesture to our two bodies for emphasis. He scowls.

"Just like that, you think you have a future?" he husks out.

Monster's big hand slides around the front of my throat, squeezing. My hands come up to pull his hand away, but he growls so loudly I can feel it where our bodies touch. The sound vibrates over my naked skin, sending out goosebumps.

"Who put such stupid ideas in your head, hmm?" He leans close, inhaling the sudden scent of my fear. Knotting his fingers in my hair, he seems almost amused. "You're going the regret asking me that, princess."

Uh oh.

His fingers tighten in my hair, making me wince. He smashes his mouth to mine, not so much kisses me as showing his dominance. He pulls on my hair again, making me gasp, and then uses that moment to invade my mouth. He licks and rolls his tongue around the entirety of my mouth, biting my lower lip until I can taste the faint tang of my own blood.

When he pulls his mouth away, I gasp for breath. He doesn't let up on his grip on my hair. Instead, he sits down on the bed, forcing my head down to his lap. I can barely open my mouth before he's shoving his cock in it, pushing my head down onto his long, thick dick.

Monster moans a little. He immediately goes deep, so deep that I gag.

"Take it," he snarls when I try to resist. "You little slut, you love it. Fuck, I love giving you exactly what you need."

The whole time, he just bobs my head up and down on his massive cock. He forces me to take him all the way to the hilt a few times. My eyes start to water, and I gag again.

He groans and leans back a little, watching my mouth traveling up and down his cock intently. There is so much saliva that it starts to drip down to the base of his dick.

For some reason, that is the thing that flips a switch

for me, turning me on. But before I can really do anything about it, he stops me.

"Enough," he grates, pulling me off of his cock. My mouth makes a satisfying *pop* sound as he pushes me off.

I can't go far though, because he moves to flip me over onto my knees. He leans down and spreads my legs, pushing my head down. As he strokes my bare inner thighs, I can feel myself grow wet.

Fuck, when Monster teases me just like this, I can't help it. I can feel his clever fingers skating over my pussy. I shiver.

He surprises me by pushing his face against my pussy forcefully. He presses his hand on my lower back and puts his mouth to my pussy, his tongue finding my clit without fail.

He circles my swollen clit a few times, then traces his tongue to my aching entrance. He delves inside. I let out a moan, pushing back against his face.

Then he moves again, pushing me down on the bed. I feel him settle against the backs of my legs, his big cock nudges my entrance. I moan.

"Yes," I whisper, closing my eyes.

He thrusts into my pussy without a second's hesitation, filling me to the hilt, stretching my pussy out in the best way possible. We both make a sound as he drives his cock all the way home.

Monster grips my hips, slamming himself into me, heedless of me. His touch is brutal, the swing of his hips frenzied. I can just barely hang on, riding the waves of pleasure building inside me.

When I come, it's sudden and unexpected and bright,

a burst of magnificent color and melodious sound. Monster is right behind me, groaning his release.

I lie still, sweat cooling on my body, struggling to pull air into my lungs. Monster flops beside me on his back, his face turned away. He's not asleep though, his eyes still open and fixed on the wall. I wonder if he is still angry about my question, or if it's something else that is bothering him.

Hesitantly, I put my arm across his chest. My head finds a natural resting spot on his shoulder. He accommodates me, moving his arm so that it is loosely around my body.

But still, he looks away.

"Hey," I say softly. He clears his throat and turns his head to me, his steely gaze probing.

"Hmm?" is all he says.

"I'm sorry. About before, I mean. When Dryas took me riding, he asked me what I had planned for the future. And I just thought... I thought that I don't know." I bite my lip.

His brows rise slightly. "Dryas put that into your head?"

I pause, then nod. "Yes. But he's not wrong. I mean, if I'm not going to die, then the future is sort of inevitable for me. For both of us."

Monster sighs a little. "Just go to sleep, Fiore."

Dejected, I start to sit up, intending to go to my room. But Monster holds me tighter.

"Stay where you are," he says faintly. He turns his head again, so I can't see his expression. Then, "Good night."

I'm floored, although I can't let out the surprised whoop of joy that is pressing at my throat. Sinking back down, I listen to the sound of Monster's breathing, smooth and deep and even. Listening to that, it's hard to think about the murky future or Monster's scheming brother.

Before I know it, I am lulled into sleep.

7

ARSEN

I watch Fiore sleep against my chest, the quiet rise and fall of her chest hypnotic to watch. Her brow is pulled down, the expression on her face one of thought. What could she be she dreaming about?

The answer comes to me easily: she is dreaming of the future. Whatever the future means to her, I suppose.

That term is amorphous. *The future*. I can't nail it down. It's ever-shifting, ever changing.

I think part of the reason that Fiore bringing it up made me so angry, is that I have been thinking of the future myself. And for the first time since I can remember, my vague view of the future has changed.

Instead of just picturing myself, my shoulders set against the unknown perils that the future might bring, I see that there are two figures. Me and her.

Where on earth did that come from? I feel like the image snuck up on me somehow, stealing into my head in the dead of night.

The thing is, I know why I get angry when she just brings it up. The issue, of course, is trust.

How am I supposed to trust her? She's tried to run away before. And it's not like she's choosing a future with me over a future with someone else. I bought her at a damn auction. I imprisoned her in my compound in Columbia. I beat her, humiliated her, did everything but rape her.

I did everything in my power to make her feel small.

So, why should she choose a future with me? I mean, obviously, I can provide a level of comfort that is rare enough.

But... that's not a reason, not really.

I look at her, at the way her thick dark lashes rest against her cheek, at the glorious golden waves of her hair.

I want her. I want her to want me. That much is obvious in itself.

But how do I just trust someone?

Maybe I need a test, a final way to tell that she is loyal without a doubt. But what would that entail?

I think for a few minutes, the sound of Fiore's breathing soothing to me.

In order to trust her, I need her to really accept who I am. Who am I?

Aside from a mob boss, I'm one thing above all else.

A killer.

A sociopath...

Or so I thought, until recently. When I started to feel things. Things that would make me vulnerable, give me a soft underbelly that could be exposed to my enemies.

Maybe if I'm truly worried, I need her to watch me work someone over. A little torture, a lot of death.

Maybe I need her to participate.

Then I will relax.

Right?

Mulling the thought over, I close my eyes.

8

FIORE

I wake in Monster's bed, alone. The sun is out, but it's still early. He's nowhere to be seen, and he didn't leave a note. Dragging myself from his bed, I return to my room and shower.

The weird euphoria I felt last night when he asked me to sleep beside him has worn away. Instead, I'm left with a sense of unease.

After all, we never really talked about the future yesterday. We had angry sex and then we passed out together. That's all.

I spend the morning lying in my bed, moping and reading. In the afternoon, I get dressed and take a walk in Audubon Park. The ancient oaks and Spanish moss are my only companions.

When I return, Jack the bodyguard is waiting for me outside, an idling SUV waiting. I purse my lips and get straight into the car, rather than talking about it. Jack gives me a thin smile.

Jack and one other bodyguard drive east first, leaving behind New Orleans.

I clear my throat, growing a little concerned. "Where are we going? I didn't really expect to be gone for very long..."

Jack looks back at me. "Mereaux."

My brows rise. The area to the southeast of New Orleans isn't really known for anything in particular. It's mostly run-down residential zones, with a few little pockets of old industrial buildings.

"Why?" I ask.

Jack sighs. "We don't know any more than you do, ma'am."

I frown, pushing back into my seat. I stare out the windows as the city grows slowly seedier, the houses more run down and farther apart. We eventually reach a little cluster of industrial buildings and slow down, turning into the car park of an old rust brown factory building.

Jack puts his phone to his ear, looking back at me. "Yeah, we're here. Yes. Okay."

He hangs up and looks at me apologetically. "You're needed inside this building. We're not supposed to escort you. Just go up the steps in the middle there."

Nodding, I chew on my bottom lip, opening the car door and sliding out. My heart begins to race.

What am I walking into, exactly?

I head up the steps, looking at the building before me. It has obviously not been regularly used in some years. Many of the window panes that stretch across much of the front are broken or cracked. I can't really see inside, because dust has accumulated on the windows.

I open the heavy metal front door, hesitating when I see how dark it is inside. When I step in and the door closes behind me, it is pitch black.

"Hello?" I call out.

I can see that I'm in a small space, separate from whatever the windows look in on. I venture forward, reaching out to feel my way along. My hands come in contact with a wall; I feel around for the doorknob, and I am gratified to open another door.

The pitch blackness fades away, leaving me in a hazy world of grayish light to see by. I step into the abandoned factory floor, squinting. The ceiling here soars overhead. There are a number of large boxy shapes the size of elephants. They are covered with gray sheets, dusty and old.

I call out again. "Hello?"

This time, Monster answers from somewhere on my left.

"Over here," he says. His voice doesn't sound far away at all.

His head appears, sticking out from behind one of the gray-sheeted boxes. His brows lift.

"Are you coming?" he asks as if I had a choice in the matter.

Clearing my throat, I start toward him. His head disappears, and I'm left to make my way around several of the ghostly shapes.

Coming around one of them, I stop in my tracks.

Monster is there, his sleeves rolled up, pondering a fair-haired man who is lying on the ground.

My mouth pulls down into a frown as I look at the man. Conscious and whimpering through the duct tape covering his mouth, he's bound with his wrists behind his back. Wrapping my arms around myself, I shiver even though it isn't cold. He looks at me, his dark eyes bloodshot, and tries to yell through the duct tape.

"Shut up," Monster mutters, pointing at him. Then Monster looks at me. "This is John. John has been very, very bad. Isn't that right, John?"

We both look at John, who tries to yell again. Monster kicks him, the sound of his foot connecting with the flabby flesh of John's gut a sickening thud that I'll never forget.

"What did I say?" Monster says, rolling his shoulders as if to release tension. "Fiore, do you know what John likes to do in his free time?"

My eyes flick to John, who is staring at me desperately. "No, obviously not."

Monster walks around John's body in slow, measured paces. "He likes to find young women. He likes to stalk them. And when they're least expecting it, he likes to break into their homes, tie them up, rape them, and strangle them. Isn't that right, John?"

A shiver erupts from the base of my spine. John shakes his head emphatically, making Monster smile.

"I have proof, of course." Monster points to a pile of ten or so cardboard shoe boxes that are neatly stacked near one of the grey ghosts. "Open one of those, would you?"

I start to tremble. There's a lump of emotion in my throat. I take careful, precise steps as I go around Monster and John, over to the mismatched boxes. All my blood is rushing fast, the sound loud to my ears.

Looking back at Monster, I reach out and take the top off of a box. Inside, there are six neat little manila envelopes, each stuffed to bursting. Tremulously, I pick up one of the envelopes. It's not very heavy. The only seal is the little metal clasp.

I look inside, seeing only papers and a few Polaroids. Curious now, I upturn the contents into my hand. I see a much-photocopied piece of paper that contains a woman's personal details: date of birth, height, weight, eye color.

Juanita Crillo. This woman is only a year older than me, brown hair and brown eyed.

The next piece of paper is the certificate of death for the same woman, the cause of death listed as asphyxiation due to ligature strangulation. I feel myself go pale as a sheet when I read those words.

I flip to the Polaroids, terror beginning to grip me. Still, I'm not prepared for the images, pictures of the last few seconds of Juanita's life as she is strangled to death, a bright red cord around her neck.

In the last Polaroid, John poses for a grinning selfie with Juanita's now-lifeless corpse. It's him, without a doubt; his hair and eyes are exactly the same, the shape of his jaw is unmistakable. My gut churn, unsettled by the way that Juanita died. I look at John, but he doesn't look at me anymore.

It's no wonder if the shoe boxes are all full of the same evidence that I just saw.

I drop the Polaroids and papers back in the shoe box, disgusted. Monster looks at me with such a smug expression of satisfaction. I want to blame him, lash out at him for bringing such a thing to my attention.

"Are you angry?" Monster says, his tone far too light for such circumstances. "You should be, I think. Does the girl's death make you hate him?"

He points to John with his foot. I flush.

"Yes," I say, point-blank. "I'm disgusted."

"Good. Use that. Fill your heart with it."

I put my hand on my hip, narrowing my gaze. "Use it to do what?"

Monster gives me the most wicked smile. "I brought John here for you. He awaits his justice at your hands. What will you do to him?"

"Me?" I say, recoiling. "Nothing!"

"Oh?" Monster says. He pulls out a switchblade, opening it to show the sharp knife to me. "Should I let him go, then?"

Juanita's frightened eyes flash in my mind, and I scowl. "No!"

"So, what then?"

He leans in, clearly expecting something from me.

"What do you want?" I ask, growing distressed.

Monster is placid. "Tell me what to do to him. Or better, do it yourself. If you don't, I will let him go."

I feel distinctly threatened by Monster's words. If he lets John go, the psychopath will be free to hunt and kill more girls. I've read stories about men like John.

They don't stop until they're dead or in jail.

But what Monster asks of me... to actually kill someone... it seems impossible. I swallow against the emotion that thickens my throat.

"Kill him," I whisper, the sound of my voice seeming loud in the silence of the old factory. "He can't do this to anyone else."

John starts making noise, pleading through his gag. I have no pity for him, though. It's all I can do not to spit on him, even though he's trussed and at my feet.

Monster raises his brows. "How?"

"How?" I echo, disbelieving. "I'm sure you know how to kill someone, Monster."

He cocks his head. "Sure, I know a dozen ways to kill him. But I want you to pick. Think of the girls, then decide."

My mouth pulls down in a frown. "You think that it needs to be reminiscent of the way he killed them?"

Monster shrugs. "Maybe. What do you think?"

I nibble on my lower lip, nodding. He flips his switchblade closed, disappearing for a moment behind one of the big gray shapes. When he reappears, he holds a length of bright red cord. I'm wracked with a shiver because it's clear that Monster brought it here with the intention of me choosing it as the method to kill John.

His lips twitch. "Nice and bloodless. Is this how you want John to die?"

I get a flash of the image of John posing with Juanita's lifeless body. The word slips from my lips, unheeded. "Yes."

Monster nods, tying the rope loosely around John's

neck so that there are two ends sticking out. He holds one and offers the other to me.

"Take your vengeance," Monster urges. "Do your worst."

I shake my head. "No. I can't."

"You can."

"Monster, I *can't*." Tears well up in my eyes.

His lips turn upward. "Such a soft little heart you have. You are certain?"

I nod, my lips numb. I lick them, anxious for this all to be over with.

Monster removes the knot, reshaping it to a noose. When he slips the noose over John's head, John starts to protest.

"No one cares," Monster informs the captive as he tightens the noose. "No one is here to see you in your last moments. I hope that I see you in hell."

Then Monster plants a foot on John's chest and starts pulling. John makes a strangled noise, his face going red right away. But he's trapped, held immobile by Monster's foot.

I look away, queasy. Monster pulls the nose harder. There is a sudden popping crunch of bone, which gives me gooseflesh all over my body.

Monster releases the noose with a flourish, looking satisfied. "It's as simple as that."

I can't bring myself to look at John's body, but Monster comes over and turns me toward him.

"Look," he urges. "See what you were a part of?"

I look at John, who has gone still. His face is still red, his head cocked a little. His eyes are open but vacant.

I start to cry, even though I know that the world should not mourn his loss. Monster embraces me, and I burrow into him, closing my eyes.

"You did well," he purrs. "Very well."

"I want to go home," I whimper.

Monster smiles at that. "That's where we'll go, then."

His arm around me, he guides me out of the factory.

9

FIORE

*T*he whole ride back to the house, Monster doesn't take his hands off of me. While he's not usually the most touchy-feely man — for from it, actually — just now he's acting ravenous for the smallest amount of my affection. He kisses my neck, running his stubble down my skin.

I demur, looking at the driver, but Monster is unconvinced.

"Don't worry about him," he whispers, kissing my ear. "Focus on me."

I submit with a sigh, closing my eyes. The second I do, Juanita and John's dead eyes come back to me. As Monster's hand comes down, sweeping aside the dark blue satin of my dress and baring my breast, I am still unsettled.

Even though he deserved it, I still essentially killed John. Standing as judge and jury, I stood by and let Monster play executioner.

What does that say about me?

I whimper as Monster pulls me onto his lap, straddling him. He pushes the other side of my dress aside, then teases me by running his hand up my thigh underneath my dress. I'm aware of how naked I am, how Monster isn't the only one who can see me.

Still, I moan softly as he toys with the top of my panties. With him, I always seem to want more of whatever he's dishing out.

"You are so lovely," Monster whispers in my ear. "And I liked what happened today. You saw what needed to be done, and you let me do it. I feel like you should be encouraged."

His fingers slip lower, nudging the flimsy material of my panties aside and brushing tantalizingly close to my clit. I let out a soft sound of pure need. He kisses me and shifts a little, hitting me in just the spot that I want.

Breathless, I writhe against his fingers, desperate to soothe the ache he's started there.

He pulls his face away from mine, watching the emotions on my face. "You're a good girl, Fiore. You know what happens to good girls?"

My breath hitches as the SUV slows. I open my eyes and see that we are in New Orleans, in our neighborhood. I shake my head, praying that he doesn't stop.

But of course, he does. He withdraws his hand as we pull up to the house. Monster leans in, his breath tickling my ear.

"Don't worry, princess. Good girls get fucked five ways to Sunday."

My heart practically flies at those words. With that, he moves me off of his lap, getting out of the car. I follow. My hand entwines with his as he leads me across the lawn and inside the house.

Once we're inside, we make it to the living room before Monster throws me on the couch. He falls on me like a starving wolf, tearing at my clothes. I'm eager too, pulling his shirt out of my pants and unzipping his zipper.

He flips me over on the couch, leaving me to hang on to the back on all fours. He presses his face between my legs and makes a mmmm sound as he finds my clit.

I cry out as he pulls my hips back toward his face, dropping to his knees. After he laves my clit, licking circles around it, he gets back up. I feel his cock press against my wetness.

"Yes," I urge him. "Fuck me, Monster."

Almost before I can get the words out, he's pushing inside me. We both groan as he thrusts the first time. He fills me up, completes me in a way that I didn't know was possible.

Oh, God... could I love him?

Could I love the Monster that enslaved me?

"Fuck, you're tight, princess," he hisses, withdrawing and thrusting again. "God, your pussy is so fucking hot, so wet for me. It's the best I've ever had."

I grip the back of the couch, tingling as much from his words as from what he's doing to my body. Maybe I have started to grow on him, too?

That's probably just fooling myself, though.

He begins to start moving faster, his thrusts wilder, more frenzied.

"Rub your clit," he orders roughly.

I slip my hand down between myself and the couch, obeying his command. My fingers trace figure eights around my clit. I close my eyes, feeling so full of him, stretched to the brim.

As I start to tighten, winding up like a spring, he continues to ram his cock into my pussy. When I'm almost there, about to come, he gasps the words I didn't know I needed.

"Come for me, princess."

I explode, my body tightening and clenching, and back bowing with my release. Monster comes as soon as I do, pounding his release into me.

Spent and sweaty, I crumble, folding my top half over the couch. Monster is not content with that, though.

He scoops me up, discarding my dress on the floor, and carries me upstairs. To my surprise, he doesn't carry me to his room, or to mine.

He carries me to the third bedroom, which was once Tony's room. It looks completely changed, though. The walls have been painted a soothing light blue, the furniture replaced with a single, giant poster bed, the four tall posts done up like a fairy's dream in frothy white hangings. There are two bedside tables too, with twin lamps.

"Monster!" I say, scolding him as he tosses me on the bed. "When did you do this?"

"Recently," he admits with a shrug. "I thought perhaps you would like to sleep in here with me."

I give him an odd look. "You're giving me an option?"

He looks uncomfortable for a brief second, then brushes it off.

"I'm tired of my bed. It's too small. Besides, it doesn't

have these." He slaps one of the posts, giving me the most wicked grin. "Just imagine what good use we will make of these, Fiore."

I get under the comforter, sinking back into the pillows. "It's perfect, Monster."

He slips in beside me. "I'm glad you like it."

He kisses my shoulder, chuckling at the tremor that runs through me. I turn my back to him, offering him the chance to spoon me. He doesn't for a minute, shifting his weight.

"Don't think that I'll be satisfied by this, just because we're in a new bed." He kisses the back of my neck, and I shiver.

"I wouldn't dare," I say.

We're quiet for a while. I start wondering what the new bedroom means because I love to overthink things.

Is it just a way for him to erase Tony more completely from the house? Or is it more than that?

"You asked about the future," He says, out of nowhere.

I glance at him, surprised. "I did."

He looks uncomfortable for a second. "I didn't handle it very well."

I shrug. "Dryas put the question in my head. Now that I think about it, it must have been to upset you."

A look of displeasure crosses his face. "Well, it was effective."

I shrug again, not knowing what else to do. "I'm sorry."

He clears his throat. "You couldn't know that it would set me off. Besides, I'm glad you asked."

I raise my eyebrows. "You are?"

He glances away. "Yes. It got me thinking about the future."

I don't say anything, wondering where he's going with this. He looks back at me, his gaze pinning me.

"I see you and me together, in my future."

My eyebrows raise again. "You do?"

He nods. "Mmhmm. And I see a change of scenery, eventually. A change of country, perhaps."

"How does that square with your job?" I ask, biting my lower lip.

He shrugs. "If I'm honest, I have lost whatever drive I had to win over the city and rule with an iron fist. I just... don't care, not the way that I used to."

I pause, thinking. "What does that mean, exactly?"

He shakes his head. "I don't know. I haven't figured it all out yet."

"Do you think you'll leave New Orleans, then?"

His steely gaze pins me. "I think that depends on a lot of factors. Would you like to leave?"

"I... I don't know. Maybe?" I reply. "I've honestly never thought about it before." I pause. "If you don't want to do your job anymore, what job would you like? Where would you want to live, if anything was possible?"

He frowns, thinking. "I don't know. This has been the only thing on my horizon for so long, it's hard to see past it."

I shift my weight, readjusting on the bed. "How long have you been doing it?"

Monster shifts too. "Since I was a kid. My brothers and I fell in with the Cypriot—"

"The who?" I ask.

"The Cypriot. The mafia, where I come from."

I trace a pattern in the comforter. "And that's Greece?"

"Cyprus," he says patiently. "Its people are mostly Greek, but the island is closer to Turkey and Syria."

He just told me, just like that. I try not to let my elation show. "I see. You said you and your brothers joined young?"

"I think I was ten at the time," he says, nodding absently.

My eyes widen. "Ten? You were a child!"

"It was a different world for us then." His mouth forms a thin line that does not beg questions. Instead, he moves to kiss my neck, his hand grasping my hip. "Enough talk."

"And what else are we supposed to do?" I tease gently.

With a growl, he sweeps my body beneath his own, and we are lost in each other for a time.

10

ARSEN

I take Fiore to the French Quarter in the bright midday sun. The bodyguards are with us, but I make sure they stay back, out of our way. She clings to my hand as we make our way to a little patisserie that I like, walking on the sidewalk, under the balconies. Almost every place is a business, advertising by hanging heavy signs overhead.

Fiore is quick to point out the funny ones, especially the one that reads "Hotel Beaucoup — Haunted and Not Haunted Rooms Available". She thinks the sign is funny, her lips lifting as she reads it aloud.

"Are the rumors of ghost hauntings true?" I ask.

She slides me a look. "It depends on whether you believe in them, I suppose. But I swear, I've been in the Lalaurie Mansion over on Royal Street and I've felt the presence of spirits. Oh, and don't even get me started on that hotel on St. Louis Street... they used to have the slave market there."

She shivers. I try not to roll my eyes. I don't believe in

ghosts. I don't believe in anything that isn't concrete. But Fiore seems entertained by telling me about the various voodoo shops around town, so I just let her without comment.

"Wait," she says, tugging my hand toward a doorway. The sign over our heads simply reads The Bakery. "This place makes the best beignets in the world."

"Is that so?" I say, cocking a brow. "I've never tried one."

Her eyes go wide. "What? Oh, you have to!"

She pulls me inside the tall wood and glass doors, insistent. As soon as I step inside, I'm nearly assaulted with the incredible scent of sweet fried dough. At one end of the cafe, there are customers standing behind a glass partition and watching the white-coated employees cut dough.

They throw it into a deep fryer, where it sizzles and pops, before dumping the beignets onto plates and dusting them with powdered sugar from a tin shaker. At the other end, the line of customers stretches to a cash register where people pay the receive fresh beignets.

Fiore pulls me into line, eagerly watching the employees work. I smile. "How many times have you seen this?"

She looks at me with a grin. "I used to come here after going to Mass every Sunday."

I raise an eyebrow. "Catholic Mass?"

Her cheeks color. "Yes. My father insisted that the whole family go. Or at least, he did before my mother died."

"I didn't realize that you were religious."

She shrugs. "I'm not, not particularly. I think that the only reason we even went was my mother. I think that having God looking over my mother's shoulder was appealing to my father."

I nod. The line moves quicker than I anticipated. I fish my wallet out of my slacks and pay the cashier for a steaming hot plate of fried dough and two coffees. I hand the two paper cups of coffee to Fiore and follow her to a little table.

It's nice here, by the windows. Bright sunlight streams in, people walk by outside. At the table next to ours, a bunch of middle school aged girls giggles over their paper cups, sliding me secretive looks. Fiore sees me noticing the young women.

"Tempted?" she asks, taking a seat.

I huff a laugh. "I think not."

One corner of her mouth crooks up in a smile. "Sure, you say that now. What will you say in a few years, though?"

She takes a beignet, cupping her hand underneath to catch the powdered sugar that falls off the top. She closes her eyes and takes a bite, letting out a *mmmm* of satisfaction. I feel as if I am being tested, even though she acts as if it doesn't matter.

Reaching out, I grab her chair and pull her close. "Give me a bite of that."

She opens her eyes and arches a brow, but she offers it to me. I take a bite, the sweetness hitting my tongue first, followed by the fatty deliciousness of the dough.

Swallowing, I sip my coffee.

"It's pretty good," I admit with a shrug. "And Fiore?"

She looks at me questioningly.

"A few years from now, I will still have my hands full with you, I think." I give her a winning smile. She rolls her eyes, but I think that the little flush I see in her cheeks means that my comment didn't go unheard.

She pushes the plate of beignets toward me. "Have another."

I do, following the sweetness with more bitter black coffee. I think to myself that Fiore and I are very much like beignets and black coffee. She's all sweetness, I'm strong and bitter.

We suit each other in a way that's every bit as strange as sugary doughnuts and coffee.

"Now I'm in the mood to spend some money," I say as we walk back outside. I look at her. "I want to see you in some expensive lingerie. Do you have any recommendations?"

She ducks her head, her cheeks glowing pink. "Maybe."

"Lead the way," I instruct.

We stroll and shop. There's plenty to see, showcased in the windows of the shops on Royal Street and Decatur Street. Art galleries, jewelry shops, antique shops. I enjoy seeing her point at things in the shop windows, commenting on whether or not they are practical, or whether or not they would be a good purchase.

She does take me into a fine lingerie shop. I insist on watching her try on some corsets and garters. To the delight of the saleswoman, I insist on buying everything that Fiore touches.

After all, what is the point of having a lot of money if you don't spend any of it?

We leave the shop, the bodyguards each carrying bags with the name of the boutique emblazoned on them. I follow Fiore as she continues window shopping, paying special interest when she stops before a pricy jeweler's shop. Though she is merely browsing, I do notice that her eye catches on a beautiful rose gold and emerald ring.

Maybe she has more plans in mind than I know about. Or maybe, given her naiveté, she's just glad to be out of the house for once. I purse my lips as I imagine Fiore wearing my ring.

Would that be the same as having her wear a collar? They are both the same shape, made of the same thing.

But one of them makes me the master, and the other makes me...

What? The husband? The partner?

My lips turn downward. "Let's go get a drink. I'm tired of window shopping."

"Sure," Fiore says agreeably, grabbing my hand again. "Whatever you want."

Whatever I want, indeed.

We head inside a place that I know, a cocktail bar named Tonique. Even though it's sunny outside, it's dark in here, making me squint for a minute as I step inside. The walls are painted black, the bar stools in ill repair, their red leather cracked. The place is small, just a horse-shoe-shaped bar and two big chalkboards listing what the specials are.

There is no one here at the moment, just a lone

bartender. The guy looks up from polishing glasses and nods to acknowledge us. I usher Fiore over to a seat, looking up at the specials listed on the menu board.

Fiore leans over to whisper in my ear. "I'm not old enough to order anything in here."

I smirk. "You'll be fine."

I pull out a couple of hundreds from my wallet, sliding them across the bar as the bartender walks over. He looks at the money, raises a brow, and asks, "What can I get you two?"

I point to Fiore. "She'll have a Ramos gin fizz. I'll have a Vieux Carré."

The bartender looks at Fiore. I can see in his face that he thinks she is too young to be drinking, but his eyes flit to the two bills I put down. He nods and turns away to begin making the drinks, no further questions asked.

He makes my Vieux Carré first, putting the finished product in a rocks glass. He then makes the gin fizz, which takes a considerably longer amount of time. When he finishes and pours the frothy confection on a highball glass, he presents it to us.

Fiore's eyes widen as she takes in the drink before her. "What is it?"

"Gin, orange blossom, lemon juice, cream, a whole egg—"

"An egg?" she repeats, screwing up her face.

"Just try it," I say, pushing her glass toward her. "You'll like it."

She grabs the straw and takes a hesitant sip, smiling as soon as the foam hits her mouth. "It's good!"

I roll my eyes. "I wouldn't order you something that you wouldn't like."

I sip my cocktail, savoring the rye whiskey and cognac. Fiore takes another sip, then looks at my drink. "What's in yours?"

"Rye whiskey, cognac, some other things. They make the best one I've ever had here."

"Here, like New Orleans?" she asks.

I smile. "No, here like this particular bar."

"Oh." She looks around, wrinkling her nose up. "It isn't much to look at, honestly."

I cock my head at her. "When you are old enough to start appreciating cocktail bars, you'll realize what a treasure this place is. That I promise you."

She drains her drink. "Can I have another one?"

I give a huff of laughter. "Sure. But do me a favor. Take it easy on this one. There is enough gin in those to get you properly drunk if you down them fast enough.

Her cheeks flush. "Okay. I wouldn't even realize that they have gin in them, if not for the name."

"Can she get another?" I say to the bartender.

I see her gaze wander again. Snaking out an arm, I pull her chair closer to mine. She smiles when I put my arm around her.

"This is nice," she says, laying her head down on my arm.

"What was your favorite part?" I ask.

She purses her lips, thinking. "Mmm.... I don't know. Maybe getting to force your first beignet on you?"

While the dour, cynical part of me expected her to say that her favorite was the lingerie shop, the secret, lighter side of me rejoices at her answer. So simple, so uncomplicated.

Could she really be as extraordinary as the image I'm slowly building in my head?

Sure not.

And yet, she says stuff like this.

Fiore gets her second drink from the bartender and sips it slowly, obviously enjoying herself. For the first time I can ever recall, I suddenly find myself wondering what someone other than myself feels.

I look at her pink cheeks and sparkling blue eyes, at her blonde hair and small stature, and I wonder if she has feelings for me.

"This part is pretty good too," she says, unbidden. She glances at me, a sly grin on her face. "It's good to spend time with you when you're not working. I like you like this, all relaxed. You should be this person more often."

"Would you fall in love with me if I were more relaxed?" I tease.

She goes as red as a beet, stammering her answer. "I... I don't know..."

My smile widens to a grin. "You feel something for me. I know you do."

She looks away, toying with the straw in her drink. "Maybe."

"Maybe what?"

She shrugs a shoulder. "I don't know. Half the time I hate you. Half the time..."

"You what? You love me?" I ask, surprised.

"No!" she protests. Then she takes a deep breath. "I don't know what I even feel the rest of the time. All I know is that I don't want you to be gone for too long. I... I start to miss you, you know?"

I sip my drink, enjoying her bashfulness. She is surprising, my Fiore. I pull her closer, enjoying this moment. She leans her head against my chest and I know a moment of happiness.

11

ARSEN

*A*fter that day in the French Quarter, I find myself wanting Fiore's company again. Needing it. Not just her body... no, I want her mind. Her soul.

I want it all.

This causes me no end of turmoil.

I think of Anna, whose presence I used to miss so badly that I could almost feel her here, even after she was dead. What would Anna think of how weak Fiore makes me?

Would she judge me, as I fear? Turn her face away from me, sneering?

More likely, she would ask when her next fix was. See, with Anna, I could never be her master because of her addiction to opiates. That came first. Heroin would always be her choice, hands down.

So, why do I keep coming back to Anna and what Anna would think, time and again?

Probably because I imagine her expression as a mirror for what I feel inside, about myself. I hate the weakness that I feel, loathe the sad suffering part of myself.

I make a sound that is part rage, part sadness. Ultimately, I bring it back to Fiore. How can a girl so small be the source of an emotion so large that it threatens to drown me?

Unfortunately, I have to work the next couple of days, putting in long hours on the Columbia deal. We are so close to closing this thing, I can practically taste it... but because it's in its final stages, my guidance is required for half a week before I can break away. I'm stuck in meeting after meeting, staring out the window.

I think of nothing but Fiore if I am honest with myself. The softness of her hair, the color of her lips, the hope I feel as handily she fits in the groove of my body after we have fucked.

I'm besotted, I realize. And that makes me angry, more than anything.

How dare she be so light and happy when I am so tortured?

When I come across an invitation to a ball, I immediately picture Fiore in a white ballgown, my band of white gold glinting at her neck. Without fully realizing what I'm even doing, I command an assistant to order the dress and let the event organizers know to expect us.

The Serpent's Society of New Orleans will get their wish to see Fiore and me at their ball. I'll be damned if I am not going to see exactly what I envisioned to take place in the real world. I even let Fiore know a day early so that she can prepare.

I head home on the day of the event, only to find

Fiore gone. A note from her lists some errands she has to do. It's as well she isn't home, because I'm in a mood.

My mood darkens considerably when Damen texts me, only a few minutes away. I think of the last time I saw him, just after he almost raped Fiore. My fists bunch, thinking of how he almost had what was mine.

I head to the front door, opening it just as he pulls up. I stride out toward him, my eyes narrowing on him, trying to gauge what he's up to.

"Brother," I say simply, inclining my head. "This is pretty last minute. You could've let me know you were arriving."

"I could have," he agrees with a smirk. "Where is your girl?"

I fold my arms across my chest and gives me a level look. "She's none of your concern, Damen."

"Still angry about the run-in we had in Columbia?"

"I'm not angry about anything." My expression says otherwise, though. "What are you here for?"

"I'm here to introduce you to my new bride." He drops the words casually as if my marriage was an expected affair.

I am honestly surprised. "Your new *what*?"

"Can we go inside?" he suggests, motioning to the house. "I don't want the details of my life broadcast everywhere. I'm certain you don't either."

I look at him for a second, my eyes narrowing. Then I back up, turning and leading the way into my house. I head into the kitchen, where I motion to a seat at the kitchen island. He sits as I grab a big bottle of mineral water and two glasses from the fridge.

"What, no alcohol?" He asks although it's only early afternoon.

I look at him and shake my head. "No. I have a social engagement later that I need to be ready for. I can have someone get you something if you want it."

"A social engagement? My, my, how the girl has changed you." I smile as he accepts the chilled sparkling water.

My brother is unamused. "What the fuck did you mean by your new bride?" I ask.

"I mean exactly what I said. She's at the Belvedere right now, getting herself settled in."

"Who did you fucking marry, Damen?" I ask, exasperated. "And why?"

He cocks his head. "Someone I've known for a while. Someone who was just waiting in the wings." He pauses. "And partly, I did it because the Tarot cards told me to. But mostly, just because she is beautiful."

My brows rise. "And am I supposed to meet this girl? What's her name?"

"Bianka. And yes. I'm hoping that whatever you and your girl have planned tonight, you can accommodate two more."

My eyes narrow to slits. "You're assuming that I am kind enough to allow you within a city block of Fiore. I left you alone with her once, and it didn't turn out well."

His lips turn upward into a smile. "Yes, I am assuming. But you haven't yet met my own bride. She's quite captivating."

"Oh?" I ask. "What are you saying, Damen? Are you offering a trade? Because I'm not interested."

I give a low chuckle. "I'm saying that I will have my hands full with my new girl. In fact, I feel like a new man with her at my side. Just like the Tarot cards promised."

I give a huff of laughter. "Again, with that? Damen, really."

He shrugs. "When it's in the cards, it's in the cards. There's nothing you can do or say."

I take a sip of my water, looking pensive. After almost a full minute, I speak. "We are scheduled to go to a ball tonight. A masquerade ball. Do you think you two can be ready for that?"

His lips twitch. "Of course. This is New Orleans, after all. You can get anything at a moment's notice, for the right price."

I am amused. "You're right about that, at least. That is what our business is all about."

Sliding off his bar stool, he stands. "When and where should we meet you?"

I consider that. "The ball begins at nine. It's at the Balconnet, just above the Treme neighborhood. I'll call and make sure your name is on the guest list."

"Very well. Bianka and I will see you then."

I watch as he leaves, finding myself extremely distrusting of my brother. Just what is Damen up to, exactly?

Fiore comes home soon after that, and I am too distracted by getting ready to mull it over further.

At eight thirty at night, I stand in the foyer, staring at the staircase impatiently. Checking my watch, I shift my weight and adjust my tuxedo tie.

"Fiore!" I call upstairs. Damn the woman, we are

going to be late. I hate the feeling of being late, the rush that inevitably accompanies it.

I look behind me, checking that the SUV is outside. When I turn back, I'm greeted by the sight of Fiore, coming down the stairs. She's wearing a white strapless ball down and the white gold collar I got for her, her hair piled atop her head.

My lips curve upward as she makes eye contact with me, grey pinning blue. She has a secretive smile when she sees me. She descends to stand in front of me, dropping me a curtsy.

"My lord," she teases.

I can't keep my hands off of her. I grab her and pull her close, bending her back to taste the sweetness of her lips. Her hand comes up to grip my lapel. She sighs into my mouth.

When I release her mouth, she grins up at me. "Are you still mad about being late?"

I smirk. "Somehow, I am not."

Tucking her under my arm, I am in no rush as we go to the car. We ride to the Treme together, me admiring the way she looks wearing my collar.

"What?" she says, blushing.

Smiling, I shrug. "I'm just looking at you. Admiring you, and how good you look on my arm. Is there a crime in that?"

She blushes redder. "No, I suppose not."

I cock my head, putting my arm around her. "I like the way you look in that collar. I'm sure that I will like it more when it's the only thing you're wearing."

She gives a laugh. "You are so..."

"Intriguing? Sexy?" I grin as I lean down, putting my lips to her ear. "Infuriating?"

I place a gentle kiss on the shell of her ear, a promise of what is to come later. She shivers. I love that she is so responsive to every little touch.

I plan to take full advantage of that later.

"No," she says, her voice coming out breathy. "I was going to say that you're so bad. But I think you know that, don't you?"

I give her my most wicked grin. "That I do."

She eyes me. "You haven't told me what to expect tonight."

"After the ball? You should expect to be trussed and fucked, I think."

Fiore slaps my hand, which creeps onto her knee. "That's not what I mean, and you know it."

I sigh, settling back in my seat. "Actually, I'm not sure. This group that's throwing the ball, the Serpent's Society? I don't know that much about them, outside of the rumors."

She cants her head. "What rumors?"

"They are swingers, I guess. Or most of their members are pansexual. Something like that."

She raises a delicate brow. "I'm sorry? They're... what, pansexual?"

"They're very open, sexually," I say, reframing it. "And they're supposed to throw a hell of a party."

She casts a doubtful eye over me. "I don't want to share you. I want to be the only one that you take home."

Something deep inside me is pleased with her declaration. I reach for her hand, stroking the back of it. "No?"

She bites her lower lip and shakes her head, coloring. "No."

Reaching up to her collar, I pull on it gently with a fingertip. "I think that can be arranged. After all, you do wear my collar, do you not?"

She gives me an uncertain smile. "I do."

I clear my throat. "I should probably tell you now that we have some guests this evening, attending the ball with us."

"Oh?" she says, her clever fingers straightening my pocket square.

"Damen is here," I intone, grasping her fingers before she can withdraw them from my chest. I see her scowl, and I'm ready for it. "Before you say anything, he has been married since the last time you saw him."

Once a bastard, always a bastard. I can divine her thoughts from here, see the change is her body language. Her brow hunches down and she looks away, her posture going stiff.

"I see."

"He's my brother," I say as if that makes any difference to her. "You have to forgive him eventually. Besides, I promise you won't be alone with him for even a second."

She looks out the window. "Forgive him for what, exactly? For trying to force himself on a girl you bought at a slave auction?"

"You're more than that," I say.

She turns her head, her eyes bluer than ever. "Am I, though?"

As I try to think of the right thing to say, the SUV

pulls up to the curb. We've arrived, in either the best or worst moment of timing I've ever experienced.

Fiore makes a soft sound of disgust and scoots over, opening the door and letting herself out. And I'm left trailing behind, berating myself for not know what to say.

12

FIORE

I'm out of the car like a shot, practically kicking the doors of the Balconnet down. The doors close behind us, and Monster and I are ensconced in a dark little room. I can hear the faint throb of music coming from beyond the doors before us.

A party rages within, it seems.

I seethe silently as we're handed masks by a footman. Of course, I should mostly be mad at myself for what happened in the car.

I slipped and forgot my place, lulled by a false sense of growing emotion. But just because I feel something for Monster, doesn't mean he has to feel anything at all for me. I forgot that for a while, but no longer.

Monster doesn't say anything as we both slip on the plain silver masks. The footman opens the door before us, and we look out into the foggy dimness. Monster puts his hand on my lower back as I step forward.

Then a second set of doors opens, showcasing the entirety of the club's main room. Though dimly lit, the room sparkles and glints with strobe lights and mirror balls overhead. The music blares, a version of *I Put A Spell on You* set to a frenzied dubstep beat.

Everywhere I look, elegant people in ballroom dresses and tuxedoes gyrate in their masks. Monster puts his hand on the small of my back again, guiding me down a few steps and right into the fray.

There is a long wooden bar lining one wall, and he steers me toward it. My eyes widen when I see two women dancing together, grinding ecstatically. They're both partially naked, their fancy dresses pushed down in the front, baring their breasts.

What kind of ball is this? I glance at Monster, moving closer to him despite being angry with him. I don't feel safe here. A couple of men writhe in time, tongues down each other's throats.

At the bar, I have a drink, something Monster calls an amaretto sour. It's actually pretty good, so I sip it while Monster looks around. I stiffen when I recognize his brother Damen coming our way, leading a waifishly thin young brunette by the hand.

Monster and Damen make eye contact, both nodding. Then Monster begins pushing me through the crowd, propelling me toward the back wall. He finds a room that's set off the main one, leading me inside. Damen and his girlfriend come in right after me, which makes me stiffen.

Monster closes the door behind the girl, turning to introduce himself.

"I'm Arsen," he says, not bothering to extend his hand to her. I catch my breath; this is the first time he has identified himself as anything other than Monster in front of me. "And this is Fiore."

I extend my hand to the girl careful not to catch Damen's eye. "It is very nice to meet you..."

She jumps in. "Bianka. Pleased to meet you. I imagine you already know Damen?"

I grit my teeth, willing myself not to bare them. "Yes, we've met."

Monster snakes his arm out and pulls me close. I avert my face, heat blooming in my cheeks. I can see Bianka trying to make a connection between Damen and me, but I just keep my mouth shut.

Monster clears his throat. "Damen's going to play nice. Isn't that right, brother?"

Damen looks to Bianka. "I've got other things on my mind. Right, Bianka?"

She smiles. "Yes, daddy. That's right."

Damen leans in and kisses her, which makes me shudder. And she just lets him... hell, I think she actually likes it.

"I need a drink," Damen says, not breaking the eye contact he's making with Bianka. "And then I need to dance with my girl."

I have never worked so hard to repress an eye roll before. Monster looks at him speculatively.

"We'll talk later," he says. He looks down at me. "I have things to attend to, but don't leave town without talking to me, Damen."

If Damen responds, I don't hear it over the sudden blare of music as Monster opens the door again. We head back out onto the dance floor.

I pull Monster to a halt, going up on my tiptoes and pressing my mouth to his ear. "I want to leave."

Monster considers that his eyes scanning my face my face for a long moment. "All right."

My eyebrows lift in surprise, but he just turns and makes his way through the crowd, gripping my hand. We discard our masks as we step out of the noisy club.

"Come on," he says, guiding my shoulders as we head away from the entrance. "The car is over this way."

It starts raining suddenly, that heavy New Orleans kind of rain. Icy wet drops, already beginning to fill the gutters as we dash to the SUV, soaking my hair and my heavy ballgown. I slide inside the door that Monster holds open for me, grinning.

When Monster climbs in, he snakes his arm around my waist. "Take us to a hotel. I want to be catered to tonight." He looks at me, his eyes glinting with a new kind of mischief. "How do you feel about ordering room service so late at night?"

Biting my lip, I lean close to whisper in his ear. "How late do you think they'll be open? I want waffles... after I work up an appetite. Any ideas on how I'm going to do that?"

He laughs, his eyes crinkling. "I can think of a few. I can tie you up. Truss you and fuck you?"

My eyes widen a little. He runs his fingertips down my arm, then up to toy with my collar. He considers me as I shiver with pleasure. "Mmm, or maybe I can dominate you in other ways? We haven't tried breath play yet..."

His fingers slide around my throat, a teasing imitation. My breath catches in my throat. I stare up at him, watching his steel grey eyes.

He smirks, drawing his fingertips down my collarbones, to my neckline. He traces the expanse of skin he finds there. "I think you'd like that too much. Would you do that with me? Maybe I could watch your touch yourself first?"

I am too excited and nervous to speak my mind in front of the driver, so I just nod. He leans down, catching my chin, and places the lightest kiss on my lips. I sigh, sinking into it, opening my mouth to his invasion. More than that, I welcome it. Beg him for it.

Demand it.

His mouth tastes sweet, his tongue finding mine. He makes a noise as he grips my arm, holding me down a bit. Dominating me with his touch and his kiss.

We pull up outside the St. Pierre hotel, a little place on the edge of the French Quarter. Inside the rather boring beige facade is a heart of gold; everything I see from the second I walk into the lobby is gold, or a mirror reflecting some gold surface.

The room is sorted very quickly, once Monster throws a wad of hundred-dollar bills onto the counter in front of the front desk person. Before I know it, we're being let into the presidential suite on the top floor. It's much classier and more subtle here than in the lobby. It's rather modern, with an elegant black bed frame taking up one whole wall on one side and a set of gray couches on the other wall. Between them, a spotless white rug stretches across the hardwood floors.

The second the door begins closing behind him,

Monster picks me up, his mouth descending to cover mine. He moves across the room. Staring up into his eyes, I am on fire for him.

I *need* him, need him to dominate me and make me feel like only he can. I giggle when he deposits me on the bed, my skirts flying everywhere.

"You laugh now," he intones, stepping back to strip off his coat. "But we'll see who's laughing when you're bent over my lap, being spanked. I know that you'll like it. I know that it'll get you wet, but you won't be laughing at me anymore."

My mouth drops open, my eyes widening. "You wouldn't."

He grins wickedly and begins rolling up his sleeves. "Oh, there isn't much I wouldn't do to you, princess."

That nickname only comes out of his mouth when I'm about to do something dirty. At the sound of it, my core tightens. Everything is suddenly sensitive; the brush of the fabric at my neckline against my breasts, the feel of the satin of my panties against the crinolines under my skirts.

The chill of the white gold collar at my throat. My fingers come up to touch it as I nervously lick my lips.

Monster considers me for a moment, taking off his shoes and socks. "Turn around. Let me help you take off that dress. You won't be needing it anymore."

My heart in my throat, I shake my head. "No."

His brows shoot up. "I'm sorry, what did you just say?"

Feeling bold, I repeat myself. "I said no. What are you going to do about it?"

He lunges forward, I let out a scream as he grabs me

by the ankles. I kick and thrash as he pulls me to the edge of the bed, turning my body over.

"No!" I protest, continuing to struggle as he throws my skirts up, baring my white lace panties. "Monster..."

He grabs me by the hips, raising them while pushing my head down. "You talk too much. Did anybody ever tell you that, princess?"

When he uses that nickname again, I grimace, pressing my thighs together. As if that was enough to stop me from making a damp spot in my panties.

I gasp as Monster grasps my panties, yanking them down around my knees.

"Mmmm, what a pretty little pussy you have," he murmurs, drawing his fingers across the back of my thighs. My core tightens as I grip the comforter.

He nudges my legs apart, spreading my pussy further for his viewing pleasure. Then he grips my hip, raising his hand. It lands with a startling smack on my ass cheek, stinging a little. I've no doubt that the impression of his hand is still there in scarlet.

"It's nice, how your ass wobbles when I teach you your lessons," he muses.

Then, without warning, he hits me again. *Smack!*

My fists bunch in the blankets. I can feel my juices start to drip from my pussy onto my thighs. I'm not sure why, but I fucking love every second of what he does to me. What he's *doing* to me now.

Smack! Smack! He hits me again and again. I find myself loving that bite of pain, leaning into it as I clamp my eyes and my mouth shut.

I almost come off the bed when he finally touches my

pussy with two fingertips, seeking out my aching clit. Fuck, that's so good.

"Ahh!" I cry, pressing my face into the mattress. I moan needily for more.

Monster unzips his pants and pushes the blunt head of his cock against my throbbing pussy. I groan and push back against him. He thrusts inside, filling me up like no one else can.

No one will ever give so much pleasure as this man does, I swear.

He grabs a fistful of my hair and rams himself into my body, again and again, being as brutal as possible. And I love it.

I live for it.

He knows my body all too well, knows from the way my pussy clenches him that I am almost there. Almost...

"Fucking play with your clit," he grits, hammering my body roughly. "Get yourself off, you little slut."

I slide my hand up and touch my clit. A few strokes is all it takes, and then I am spasming around his cock, screaming into the comforter.

"Fuck!" he whispers, his voice gone to gravel. "You're going to make me come."

A few seconds later he tenses then slams into me, his voice hoarse as he bellows his release. He withdraws and sinks down onto the bed next to me, his eyes closing.

I scoot a little closer, and his arm comes up, automatically sliding around my shoulders. We lay like that for a long time, our breathing ragged.

13

FIORE

*I*n the early hours before dawn, I am sick. I wake up with my stomach in a tumult, vomit rising in the back of my throat before I even open my eyes. Plastering my hands over my mouth and running to the bathroom, I barely make it to the toilet before I retch up all the waffles from last night. I kneel before the toilet, tears streaming down my face, and silently gag for twenty minutes.

Afterward, I feel headachy and lightheaded, so I just sit by the toilet for a long while. It's cold on the floor. I'm not wearing a stitch of clothing, not since Monster stripped me of it earlier. All I have is the collar, and that won't keep me warm. I pull a towel off the counter, sitting on it.

I'm not sure what made me sick. I'm usually not sensitive to anything. It must have been the waffles, although how you make waffles bad is beyond me.

When I finally get up and rinse my mouth in the sink,

I hear Monster's faint call from the other room. "Are you alright?"

I pad out of the bathroom, giving him a sheepish look. "I'm fine. I think something was weird with the waffles I ate, that's all."

Monster pulls back the covers, making a space for me. I settle back on the bed, comfortable in his arms. Soon the warmth makes me drowsy enough that I close my eyes, drifting off.

I open my eyes again to find myself staring at Monster's place in bed. It's dawn, or almost... the faint light in poking slits in the curtains that Monster drew close over the windows. I sit up with a yawn, looking for him. I find him at the desk, staring down at the phone in his hands.

He looks *worried*. I don't think I've ever seen Monster look worried before this moment.

He glances up, seeing that I'm awake in the mirror in front of him. He doesn't move, just keeps looking at me. The frown lines bracketing his mouth deepen.

"What?" I ask, tousling my hair. "What is it?"

"That was Damen, just now. He said that our house..." He stops and swallows. "He said that our house is gone."

My jaw drops. "What... what do you mean, gone?"

I've heard of houses disappearing in the hurricanes, but not in this weather we're having tonight. It might've rained for all of twenty minutes earlier, but now it's promising to be a beautiful late fall day.

I'm honestly not even sure that I heard him right.

He clears his throat. "He said that there was a fire. Not

a naturally occurring one; he meant someone started a fire that demolished the house. It's just... gone."

My hand comes up to my throat, feeling for my collar. "I... I don't know what to say. God, are the servants okay?"

His face wrinkles for a moment. Is he worrying about them, or wondering why I'm even saying anything? With Monster, it's impossible to tell. "I don't know."

"We should check on them. We should see the house," I say. A thought occurs to me and I look to Monster, horrified. "Thank god that Cerberus is still at that training camp you insisted he go to."

I feel winded like I just can't quite get my breath. When I imagine that great old house being nothing but a pile of smoking rubble, I want to cry.

"Hmm," he says, looking out the window. "The club we were at last night, The Balconnet?"

I look at him expectantly. "Yes?"

"There was a mass shooting there, too."

My eyes go wide. "So... this fire..."

He finishes my thought. "It wasn't an accident, no."

I feel the same kind of queasiness that I felt this morning. The same bitter bile, backing up into my throat. I collapse backward in the bed, feeling strangely hollow.

"People are after us," I whisper, closing my eyes. "How does that happen, exactly?"

When he doesn't answer after a minute, I turn my head and open my eyes. Monster looks pensive, gazing out the window. His dark hair is slightly flattened on one side, his normally dewy and dusky complexion has gone a bit pale. He has dark circles rimming both eyes.

He looks human, I suddenly realize. He looks worried. That means we have something to be afraid of.

"Monster," I say, calling his attention away from the window. He looks over at me, his grey eyes serious.

"What?"

He sounds a little lost, although there is an undertone of anger there too.

I start to cry. I can't help it. "What are we going to do? Where are we going to hide?"

He sighs, getting up and coming to sit beside me. "Look at me. Look at me, okay? That is not for you to worry about. You're going to be safe and well cared for, no matter what."

I don't like how distant he makes that sound. As if I will be cared for after he's murdered. Pushing myself up, I throw myself in his arms, hiccuping and sobbing.

"No! I just found you. Don't say that *I* will be taken care of... tell me that *we* will be okay." It sounds hysterical, probably because it is. "Promise me!"

His hands descend on my back, comforting me.

"I can't tell you what I'm not certain about myself," he says quietly.

My hands tighten into fists and I pound them into his chest. "You have to promise me. You don't understand!"

His hands are soothing on my back, smoothing back and forth in a rough arc. "What don't I understand, Fiore?"

I gulp. The words are out of my mouth before I even think about what they truly mean. "I love you, damn it. I can't lose you!"

Monster freezes for a long second, then his hands start rubbing my back again. "You don't know what you're saying. You're upset."

I push off of him, willing him to see the truth that is written plain on my face. "I'm upset, but that doesn't change anything. I still love you."

His expression is just short of incredulous. "You can't."

"I can!" I say, my jaw squaring. "I do. I may be young, but I know my own mind. I love you, Monster."

He pulls away from me, getting up to walk to the window. His face is grave. "I hope you don't expect me to say it back to you."

I recoil just a little, stung by his words. "No. I don't."

But a little part of me is angry that he doesn't. Am I the only one who feels this way when we're together?

That's a fact that I had not considered. It certainly weighs on me now.

"We're getting off track," he says blearily, wiping his hand over his face. "I have to focus on the house being burned down and the shooting at the club. I don't have time for this... this... whatever this is."

He's so damned dismissive, but he's also sort of right. I'm definitely not done talking about the issue, but there are other more immediate concerns at the moment.

I wipe my face with the sheet, sitting up. "Let's make a checklist. Or a list of priorities."

Monster turns his head a little to look at me. "Yeah?"

I slide out of bed, pulling the sheets off and tucking the ends around myself to make a toga. "It's what my mother used to do when a situation was overwhelming. Make a list, then start ticking things off. Do you know where you want to start?"

"Mmm." He considers that. "Well... I guess I'd start by getting all my bodyguards here. Then I'd dispatch a couple to do reconnaissance on the house, find out if the servants made it out or not. If they did, I'll need to track them down, because they might know something helpful." He shrugs. "That part is easy enough."

"What's next on the list?" I ask, grabbing the comforter and pulling it over my shoulders for warmth.

He sighs. "We have to assume that this is motivated by my business. Who would be upset that I'm about to close the deal here in New Orleans?"

I frown. "I don't know. A rival gang, maybe?"

Monster slides me a curious look. "Yeah, maybe. Somebody that isn't getting a cut, I guess. Maybe one of the factions that were forced out of New Orleans when I took over."

"Makes sense to me," I say with a shrug.

His expression grows conflicted. "I don't think you're going to like this, but I am going to have to go out."

"Like hell you are!" I utter sharply. "What, are you going to lead the murderers away from me? What if they're after me, and you leave me alone?"

Alright, that isn't my real concern, but it's real enough to get my point across. I can see the war of emotions as they play out on his face.

"Fiore, this is very serious. Dangerous, if you get down to it."

"And what isn't, exactly? Because if you'd left me to sleep alone tonight, I would have probably died in that house fire."

He flinches at that. There is some satisfaction in knowing that even if he doesn't feel the same way that I do, he doesn't welcome the idea of my demise. It may be pathetic, but I'll take any little scrap of good news right now.

"It's hard to know what to do," he says at last. He hangs his head. "Just tell me what to do."

I walk over to him, putting my arm around his waist and resting my head against his shoulder.

"Focus on everything else, not on me. Just assume I'm going to come with you, at least as far as staying in the SUV. Then we're mobile. It's harder to hit a moving target."

His forehead wrinkles as he looks down at me. "That's true."

I hate to see him so lacking in motivation. "How about we start by ordering some new clothes be brought here? That will give the bodyguards time to gather."

He nods, tense. "I'll get someone grab you something that's wearable for tonight. Tomorrow, we'll worry about dressing you properly."

I give him a smile. "Sounds good."

Monster leans closer to my embrace for a moment, then pulls away. He puts his phone to his ear, issuing commands almost immediately.

A few hours later, he convenes a meeting of the body-guards in the little sitting room. Although I'm dressed now, wearing some new bright pink Juicy Couture sweats, I stay out of the room. Monster has enough to deal with without worrying about me today.

He leaves his phone in the bedroom though. I know, because as soon as he goes into the other room, his phone lights up on the bedside tables, a text message crossing the screen.

Sorry about your loss, it says. It's from Dryas.

I purse my lips, choosing to ignore the message. Monster will see it when he comes back from his meeting.

But of course, that's not all that Dryas has to say.

Are you reading this, Katherine?

And, of course, you are. Are you scared?

I whip my head around, looking at the window. I stalk over to it, peering out into the morning sunlight. Across from the hotel is another four-story building, though it appears vacant. I search the windows but see no one.

How is Dryas looking at me? Maybe he's not really looking, and he's just hoping that I will get paranoid.

The phone buzzes again. I'm drawn like a magnet to see what it says.

Nice sweat suit. Very flattering.

Ice cold water fills my veins. I run over to the window, yanking the curtains closed. Shaking, I jog over to the door where Monster is having his meeting, listening in.

Can I interrupt him? Is it worth it?

Fuck it. I barrel into the meeting, careening straight for Monster's arms. He may not think of his brother as a threat, but I definitely do.

After today, I start to wonder just what he's doing in town... so close to a mass shooting and our house burning down.

Monster's arms close around me, and for a minute, I feel safe again.

14

FIORE

I'm afraid. I think I have a right to be, at this point. It's been two days now since our house was destroyed, and we haven't made a bit of progress yet. I sit in the SUV, chewing my nails down to the nubs, waiting for Monster to come out of some house in the Eighth Ward. Not any old house, but a drug dealer's house.

Or that's my best guess, anyway. Judging by the fact that there's a guy with a machine gun out front, casually holding it and drinking an orange Big Shot with his free hand.

What Monster should be doing is trying to figure out where the heck his brother is. While he just rolled his eyes and claimed that Dryas was just messing with both of us, I'm not so sure. Those chills down my spine felt awfully real to me.

I shift in my seat, clearing my throat. Jack looks back at me from the passenger seat, unimpressed.

"You need to calm down, Miss Fiore. You're making

me nervous, you hear?" He looks back out at the house, taking in the young man with the gun.

"I'm sure that you're used to all this, huh?" I ask. Jack just grunts, noncommittal. "Driving around to drug dealer's houses... this is new to me."

Jack looks at me and sighs. "It's not part of my usual routine if that's what you're asking. Homie over there looks like he's barely awake, yet he's strapped. That shit makes me nervous."

I nod, looking out the window at the guy we're talking about. "He's awfully casual about it."

As I watch, the front door opens. Monster comes out, followed by one bodyguard. The dark circles under his eyes are even more pronounced than they were yesterday. When he slides into the back seat beside me, I see him wiping what looks like blood off of his knuckles.

Raising my eyebrows, I nod to his knuckles. "I assume it got violent, then?"

He nods, looking tired. "Yep."

"And?" I prompt.

He looks out the window, a sigh on his lips. "I got the name of someone who is reasonably certain to have been involved."

"According to the person you just... interrogated?" I point to the cuff of his coat, which has a smear of blood on it.

He doesn't react other than flicking his cuff so that the blood lands in a blob on the back of the passenger seat. "Yes. At least I've got a name. Arturo diSlava, who is tangentially connected to the Salvadorian mafia. We drove them out when we rolled into town. We can keep pressing forward with that."

"So, where to next, then? Or have you realized that you do have to sleep sometime?" I reach up, stroking the hair back from his temple.

He leans into my touch for a second, his eyes closing. "I can sleep when I'm dead."

My lips twitch. "I see."

Monster speaks up. "Driver, take us to the Penthouse Club. It's just off Bourbon Street, on Iberville Street."

A strip club? I can only hope that Monster's business there will be brief.

The SUV pulls out. Monster is quiet, thinking God knows what. I slip my hand into his, entwining them. He looks at me, those grey eyes of his shining, speaking of unknown depths.

I grip his hand, letting him know without words that he can rely on me. That I am here for him, no matter what.

He smiles a little, squeezing my hand back. The SUV navigates us to the French Quarter, pulling up outside a trashy neon sign declaring it to be the Penthouse Club. It's only early evening, not even six yet, but already there are half-dressed girls hanging out of the Club's doors.

"I'll be back," Monster says with a sigh.

My brow knits. "Can I come with you?"

"In here?" he asks, looking at the Club. "I mean... sure. I guess it's not going to be anything you haven't seen before."

I shake my head, climbing out of the SUV. It's only a few short steps to a waiting bouncer, who asks for our identification. The handoff of a hundred bucks from Monster to the doorman is so smooth, I almost don't catch it.

"Go ahead," the door guy says, stepping aside.

"Thanks," I say, going through the tall wooden doors.

Monster is right on my heels, blinking at the ill-lit space. Jack, the bodyguard, is behind him, the other one staying with the car.

It's louder than I expected here, a popular rap song booming. First, we have to walk through the marble-topped bar area, where a bartender pours a beer for her sole patron. Then we come out into the main room. It consists of two platform stages for the dancers, with a sea of little tables in between the two, pairs of heavy green plush chairs pushed up to them.

There are only a few people here, men who are already drunk. On the main stage, one brunette strips lazily. A stick-thin blonde in a pink G-string gives one of the patrons a lap dance.

I look to Monster, who scans the whole room. I only notice the second floor of private dance rooms because I follow his gaze there. He jerks his head toward the stairs.

"That way."

I follow him up the dark carpeted stairs, taking everything in. This is my first time in a place like this, so I have plenty to look at. He pauses when he sees the back hallway, with its employees only sign.

"I think you should stay here," he says, his expression hardening.

"They burned my house down too," I remind him gently.

He looks at me for a second, then nods. "All right."

We head down the innocuous looking hallway. It's beige, with unmarked beige doors. Monster pauses outside each doorway, leaning close to listen. What he's hoping to hear, I have no idea.

On the fourth door, his hand goes up. "Here, I think."

He looks to Jack, nodding to the door. Jack takes the door down with one big booted foot, and it crumples beneath his assault. Feminine screams issue from inside the room. I move to get a glimpse of girls in their panties, standing around a table and packaging up little baggies of white power.

At Jack's intrusion, the girls put their hands up as one, stepping back from the table. This isn't the first time they've been interrupted doing this kind of work if I had to guess.

"Where's Arturo?" Monster asks, seeming almost bored. "I don't want any of you. It's him I have the beef with."

One of the pretty Latina girls points to the next office. "He's there."

His smile is thin and dry. "Thank you. I'm going to leave my girl here to look after you, so behave."

Me? I try not to look so shocked. He and Jack storm out of the room. As I stand here, looking at the young Latina girls, I hear the door being breached and several men yelling in Spanish.

"Who is he?" one of the girls asks me, jerking her chin toward Monster.

"Arsen Aetós. He's taking over New Orleans." I shrug.

"Sorry to interrupt your work day. We'll be done soon, I imagine."

And I'm not wrong about that. After a lot of loud swearing in Spanish and some screaming, Monster pokes his head in the room.

"We're leaving," he says as if he was just telling me the time.

Shrugging awkwardly at the girls, I follow them out. Monster hustles me down the hallway and outside, his expression grim.

"What, did you not get what you wanted?" I ask.

Monster puts his finger to his lips, making eye contact with me. The SUV pulls up and he practically shoves me inside before he gets in and closes the doors.

"Drive," he orders, barely glancing at the driver. To me, he smiles. "We got what we wanted. The names of some places where Arturo spends time, and some people connected to him."

"Should we go back to the hotel?" I suggest gently. "I'm tired."

Not a lie exactly, although not entirely true. It's just that Monster is looking ragged. I'll say I need sleep if it means he'll rest too.

I look at him, see the wheels turning behind his eyes. Reaching out, I place my hand on his thigh and bite my lip.

"Please?" I ask. "I need you. I need you right *now*."

His eyes flash. "Driver? Back to the hotel."

We're close to the hotel, and it isn't long before Monster is carrying me into our suite. His touch is like fire, burning into my skin. I didn't lie, after all.

I do need him.

The early evening slides away, passing in a blur of mouths and tongues, groans and murmurs. Long after we've fucked twice, we lie in bed, drowsing together.

His lips are on my neck, half of his face buried in my hair.

"Your skin is so soft," he says, whispering into my skin. I shiver and stretch, smiling. "How do you do that?"

"I bathe in the blood of young virgins," I tease lightly, looking over at him. His hand skims down my bare hip, slipping beneath the sheets that I wrapped myself in.

He touches the top of my thigh, next to my pussy. Swirling his fingertips there, his lips finding a sweet spot on my neck, he is tempting me to initiate another round of intense sex. I know him by now, know how he operates.

I can read his mind, at least where my body is concerned.

"It's working," he comments idly. Sliding his hand around to cup my ass, he makes a satisfied noise.

I turn over to face him, cupping his cheek with one hand as I press my lips to his. To my surprise, he doesn't take control right away. Instead, he seems content to let me set the pace.

My heart starts to thud when I find myself wondering if this is what normal people do. Is this how you kiss when you're in love? Slow and passionate, like you'll have all the time in the world with your lover?

I release his lips, leaning my forehead against his. He smiles and pulls my body closer.

"Mmmm. I wish we could stay like this forever." The

words leave his lips, but they could easily have been my own.

I'm careful not to make a fuss. The last thing I want is to make a dramatic scene about how something special is definitely growing between us. I don't want to scare Monster away.

Let him figure it out on his own. It's better if he thinks the idea is his and come to terms with it, I think.

So, I lie here, being gently touched by Monster, and I don't smile.

But I want to. And I think one day soon, I will be able to without repercussions.

15

ARSEN

*I*t's late when I come back to the hotel. Fiore is already in bed, but she turns on the lamp on the bedside table when I return. Sitting up in the bed, she pats a spot beside herself.

"Come here," she murmurs, yawning a bit. "Come sit. Or even better, get undressed and sleep. You have been going for days now with a few hours' sleep at a time. I worry about you."

My lips twitch as I take my jacket off, heading over to sit beside her on the bed. She's warm from being under the blankets. I hook my finger in the blanket at her thigh, tugging it aside to reveal nothing beneath but bare skin.

"Monster!" she protests, swatting at my hand. But I can tell she really doesn't mean it. "Where have you been?"

I pull her naked body onto my lap, blanket, and all. She squeaks.

"Hey!" she says. Again, she scolds me, but her tone is

missing the sharpness. I bury my face in her collarbone, what little of it there is.

"I found us a better place," I say it against her flesh, making her writhe. I cup one of her full breasts, squeezing it, and then put my lips around her nipple.

Her response comes out breathy, a sound I can't get enough of. "You did?"

"Mmhm," I say, distracting myself by pulling her whole body around so that she straddles me. There's a blanket in between us, and I feel like that's far too much.

Grabbing the blanket with my fist, I yank it roughly out from under her. She gives it up with a sigh, resting her forearms on my shoulders.

I'm already hard, and Fiore is tantalizingly close to rubbing her pussy over my cock. My brain automatically estimates that the layer of clothing between us can disappear in seconds.

Fiore presses her ass down onto the tops of my thighs. Her nipples are already hardening. I hear her soft moan, which I swear I could hear for the rest of my damn life.

If I had to choose one thing to listen to, it would definitely be that moan. Or, maybe the one that means I'm balls deep inside her, and she's about to come.

That one is not to be missed either.

I sigh because this isn't what I'm here to do. "I'm supposed to be bringing you to the new place as we speak."

She pauses, the war between her hunger for me and her desire to get out of this hotel room playing across her face. She's so expressive. I can always read her whole body like a book. "Right now?"

I drop a kiss on her shoulder and nod. "Right now."

Her head cants. "Will you stay with me for a while to help me get to know the new place?"

She thinks she is so clever, asking for a favor when she really means, am I going to stay and fuck her tonight. I smile indulgently. "Yes, princess. I am going to make sure you have everything you need, you can bet on that."

The look in her baby blue eyes when I call her that nickname is unmistakable. The way she nibbles on her pink lower lip just so...

I have to push her off of my lap because otherwise, I'm going to fuck the hell out of her. And I know that she would want it. Encourage it.

Maybe even scream my name when I made her come.

Moving her to the side, I get up. "We can fuck all night long as soon as we get to the new apartment."

Her eyes twinkle. How does she look so damn good sitting there wearing nothing at all? "Is that a promise?"

Walking toward the door, I call back to her. "Or a threat, if you prefer."

I get her into the car, finally, once she's fully dressed. We drive up Canal Street, heading for a big block of brand-new apartments, six stories high and made of brick. I see her scoping them out as I help her from the car.

"This is where we're going?" she asks, a little confused.

"Just wait," I tell her. "Come on, I'll take you to the elevator."

I walk her to the building, swiping a little plastic identification tag at the door. I hand it to her as we go inside to the bank of shiny new elevators.

"It will get you in the door," I call the elevator, and then once inside I grab her hand and swipe the tag again over a metal box. "You need it here, too."

I push the button for the sixth floor and the doors close, carrying us upward. When we reach the floor, she steps out first into a blank white room. Other than a bench and a window on either side of us, there isn't much other than the door immediately before us... and a body-guard, suited up in all black swat gear.

Fiore looks back at me for a second, unsure. But then the bodyguard sweeps to the side, using a keypad to open the door. It slides open with an electronic beep, and the guard waves us on.

"Fancy," Fiore mutters as she heads through the door.

On the other side, is an open concept loft. With high ceilings, huge windows lining the walls, and cement walls and floors, it's been designed by someone with a love of modern furnishings.

To the left, a kitchen and island, all done in polished stainless and the same cement as the whole apartment. To the right, my office and a living area with big white furniture are separated by soaring red-paneled dividers.

More dividers indicate the bedroom. Best of all, though, is the rooftop view.

I glance at Fiore, whose mouth is hanging open. "Come here. Come to see the outside."

I walk her over to the all-glass French doors next to the kitchen, opening them excitedly. I step back and let

Fiore see that the rest of the floor is taken up by a charming outdoor patio, including a little lap pool.

"I... I don't even know what to say..." she gasps, bringing her hands to her mouth. She seems to be at a loss, coming over and hugging me, still awestruck. "Did you rent this?"

I cock my head. "You know I don't believe in renting. I bought the whole building, with a mind to rent this space out if we move again."

"Jesus," she says, walking over to the side of the building and looking down. "It feels like some other city until I look down on the oak trees and the streetcar running up and down the way."

"That's only part of the point. Do you like it?" I ask.

"Monster... I absolutely love it," she says, looking at me with her baby blue eyes. I see a shimmering of tears just starting there. "Really, it's perfect."

She goes back indoors. I follow her as she takes it all in, her eyes wide. The front door opens, and I hear nails clicking for a moment before Cerberus makes an appearance, looking as black and curly as ever.

"Cerberus!" she exclaims, kneeling on the floor and hugging the excited puppy. "I'm so glad to see you! Yes, I am. Yes, I am!"

They play for a few minutes before Cerberus starts sniffing around, whining to be let outside. I crack open the door for him, letting him come and go as he wishes.

Fiore hugs me hard after I let Cerberus out. "Thank you."

I shrug, keeping my reactions casual. I'm glad to see

her so delighted by everything, though. The last week has been hard on me, but it's been rough for her too. I saw it in her eyes, heard it in her voice.

She wipes at her face. "I guess I should see everything, huh?"

When she gets to the bedroom area, a big white curtain hangs by the window. Centered there is a pale pinkish-purple velour bed with crisp white sheets, two light wood bedside tables paired with two matching stainless-steel lamps beside it.

She pauses as her eye catches on the lamp, just the way I intended it to. There is a fine gold collar attached to the base of one of the lamps. There's a length of finely wrought golden chain snaking up the lamp's stainless-steel spine.

The very same chain and collar that she found wrapped around her own neck when she awoke at my house in Columbia.

She must feel something because her hand goes to her heart. When she looks back at me, I see that she's out and out crying.

"I don't know why that makes me sentimental, but it does," she laments, wiping her eyes on the back on her hand. "I almost want to tell you to go to hell with all of this. It's too much, Monster."

I sidle up to her, putting my arm around her. "Come test out the bed with me."

She gives a choked laugh. "You would say that, wouldn't you?"

I draw her over to the bed, falling onto the mattress.

Fiore catches sight of the collar again and starts crying anew. I don't mind. I expected her to react emotionally, though I wasn't sure which emotion she would feel. I also didn't expect her to react so *much*, honestly.

So, I'm happy to hold her for a bit, letting her cry all over my white dress shirt. As I lie there, my right foot falling asleep because I don't want to shift her into a different position, it suddenly becomes startlingly clear to me.

I love this girl. I must if she is so dear to me that I would go through any measure of discomfort for her sake.

Glancing at her messy blonde hair and puffy eyes, all I want to do is smile. That and cheer her up, so I can ravage her. The ache that I feel is with both my heart and my libido; I want her, as I have never wanted anyone before.

I want her love. I want her company. I want all her time; with her smiles, and her tears. I want to always look over and find her there, right by my side.

I fucking *love* her.

That's not what comes out of my mouth when I try to say something to her, though. I clear my throat. She looks up.

"Arsen," I say gruffly. "That's my first name."

Wiping away an errant tear, she smiles gently. "I know."

How long has she known, I wonder? Shrugging uncomfortably, I say, "You can use it if you want."

She gives me a knowing look. "I may if the situation

warrants it. But I find I'm quite fond of Monster. Aren't you?"

My lips lift a little. "Yes, I suppose I am."

She settles on my chest again. For a while, we're both quiet. I'm wondering how she knew my name. Did one of my brothers tell her? It seems likely.

She looks up at me, hesitating. When she speaks, her voice is almost too soft to hear. "I know about Anna too."

My eyebrows shoot up. I slide out from under her, needing a little space to breathe. "What? How?"

She bites her lower lip, glancing down at the bedspread. "I saw a picture of you two together. Then later, your brother told me about her. I put the pieces together."

I stand up, pacing to the window. "And what pieces did you put together, exactly?"

She doesn't look up. "I know... I know you cared for her." She hesitates again. "I know we have some of the same features, somehow. She looked like me, in the picture I saw. And... I know that she died. Died horribly, from what I heard."

My fists clench. I turn back toward her, gritting my teeth. "That won't happen to you, Fiore. Anna's death was my fault, but—"

For the first time since I've known her, she interrupts.

"It wasn't your fault unless you killed her," she says, picking at the comforter beneath her body.

I stride over to her, tilting her chin to look up at me. "I swear, I didn't."

She shrugs, not resisting. "Then you didn't kill her. I

don't want to hear you say you did, ever again. You can take responsibility for plenty, but not that."

I kiss her, pushing her back on the bed. Foolish little girl, trying to absolve me of all my sins. I'd teach her otherwise, someday.

Not tonight, though. Tonight, I will just be lost in Fiore. That's enough, for now.

16
─────

FIORE

I walk around a big display table, feeling the different weights of the sweaters. This is one of those froufrou stores that basically has the industrial vibe of my loft, but with many tables of expensive jeans and sweaters that are incredibly soft to the touch. I'm aware of my bodyguard walking too closely behind me. A new guy named Elian.

I turn, a smile plastered on my face. "Do you mind not being quite so close?"

Elian just shrugs his big, muscular shoulders. "Mr. Aetós wants you to be safe."

I lose my patience. "I promise, you can keep me safe from four feet further away from me."

A tall figure steps into the store. I look over to find Dryas, looking pleased. "Did I just interrupt you having a little hissy fit, my darling?"

I go cold all over, my temper flare forgotten. Dryas showing up here is a distinct threat, otherwise, he would've turned up when Monster was around.

I look at Elian, beginning to feel sweat break out across my temple. "We need to go."

"Uh, uh, uh, not so fast!" Dryas says, putting his hands up. "I just came to talk. I promise."

Elian moves toward Dryas with an angry grunt, spreading himself out as tall and broad as he can make himself. Dryas isn't worried. He pulls back his jacket, showing that he has a gun in his holster.

"Don't fuck with me," he says levelly, looking first at Elian and then at me. "If I was here to do something violent, I would've already done it. As I said, I'm here to talk."

Though I'm suspicious, I don't want Dryas to pull a weapon in here. This little shop is not ready for what would happen thereafter, I don't think. "Elian, it's okay. Just stay right here, so I can shop."

The smug look on Dryas's face makes me grit my teeth. He smiles at me. "That's a good girl. Are you always so obedient?"

I put my nose in the air, turning away. I pick up a pair of jeans, checking out the wash. "Why are you here, Dryas?"

"Arsen called a meeting of the three brothers later today. He has some news, apparently. Do you know what sort of news he has?"

I refold the jeans, perusing the stacks of t-shirts instead. "I am certain I have no idea. If you're worried, you should be talking to him."

Dryas clicks his tongue. "I think that he's about to announce that he's going to cede New Orleans to one of us, in order to keep his pretty new bride to be happy and healthy. What do you think about that?"

I pause, my hands gripping a t-shirt. I still don't look at Dryas, though. "I hate to repeat myself, Dryas. I have no idea about what Arsen has planned."

His smile thins. "No? Well, no matter. I'm here to make an offer."

I roll my eyes, heading to another table of cosmetics and perfumes. "I can't imagine what you would offer that would tempt me."

"Make the bodyguard back off, and I will tell you."

I look at Dryas. I don't see any signs of deception on his face. What could it hurt? I sigh, turning to my bodyguard. "Elian? Stand by the front door, please. Don't make a scene, and we'll be on our own much faster."

The big bodyguard doesn't emote. He just thinks for a second, then turns and heads to the front door. It's only fifty feet away, so I feel safe still. I keep on moving, circulating amongst the tables.

Dryas just follows me, persistent. It's like have a tall, menacing shadow. "I'd offer you a great deal of money. A new name. A new life, somewhere far away from here. All you would have to do is disappear. Leave and be gone without a trace. With my help, of course."

I glance at him, my brow scrunching. "What? Why?"

He sighs, reaching over to pick up a silver powder compact. "Because. I have a plan for my brother, and you don't factor into the equation. My plans are bigger and better, but they don't include someone for him to worry about. It's essential to my plans that Arsen doesn't have..."

He pauses, searching for the right words.

"What, anyone to live for?" I say. I don't bother to hide the sarcasm in my tone.

Dryas looks at me like he would look at a pervasive insect of some kind. Something to be gotten rid of, not something to consider as a part of Arsen's life.

Then again, seeing how I came into Arsen's life originally, can I really blame him?

"Any attachments," he says, finishing his thought. "And you are the very definition of an attachment, even if you're not willing to be sold again. So, I figure that if it's not a man you really crave, it must be freedom."

I snort. "And that's what you're offering me, huh? Freedom?"

He shrugs. "Of a sort. You can go anywhere outside the places where the Aetós brothers have strongholds. Do anything you like or nothing at all. You'll have the means to be anyone, as long as you keep your profile low." He pauses, then adds, "And you'll keep our agreement secret, of course."

I allow myself to imagine it, just for a second. It's silly, but I picture myself in Morocco, dressed in a loose flowing caftan and exploring ancient ruins. I can almost feel the sun on my face, feel the desert winds at my back as I walk through the desert landscape.

My lips twist. I would have to leave Monster behind for any type of arrangement to be made... and I don't think I can do it. Besides, if Monster is really going to announce that he's giving up New Orleans, we could possibly go to Morocco together.

Or any damn place we want to go, honestly.

I turn to Dryas. "I don't think so."

His expression darkens. His hand snakes out, catching my wrist. His fingers squeeze my flesh uncomfortably tight. "Is that right? That's too bad."

I try to shake him off, frowning. "Only from your perspective. Let me *go*."

Instead of letting me go, he draws me closer, grabbing my chin. His grip is bruising, punishing. "You're a stupid little girl, meddling in affairs you don't even understand. My brother cannot leave New Orleans. Do you hear me?"

His raised voice draws Elian, who comes at a run. He's not fast enough for Dryas, though. Dryas pushes his mouth upon mine, holding my chin. His lips bruise mine. I try to push him off of me, but I'm ineffectual against him.

He releases me and steps back just as Elian reaches us. He puts his hands up in surrender, his mouth quirking up just like Monster's does when he's being bad. He stares at me, never breaking eye contact with me though he addresses my bodyguard.

"Okay, okay," he says as Elian jostles him. "Listen, I'm going. I'm going, okay?"

Elian grabs Dryas and hustles him out of the store. I'm left shaking, assuring the store's lone sales associate that I am perfectly okay. And I am, though I'm determined not to see Dryas again.

It's one thing for him to call me names, it's quite another for him to lay his hands on me and kiss me. That's over the line, whether Monster thinks it's okay or not.

I clear my throat and continue with my shopping,

determined not to let Dryas ruin my day. I go to a few more stores, though I don't buy anything.

Then as I'm about to get back into the SUV, I see the drug store. Although I'm not sure what can be done for bruises, I'm interested in looking. Maybe there's something new that will take the bruises away from my lips and jaw, and maybe my wrist too.

I head down the brightly lit aisles of the convenience store, browsing as much as anything. While there isn't anything new for bruises, I do grab a couple of shades of makeup. That should cover some of it, anyway.

Then I head to the register, stopping short when I reach the feminine hygiene aisle. I should need tampons. Actually, I should've needed tampons a month ago.

How insane has my life been that I am standing in the drug store, trying to calculate when my last period was?

I grab some tampons, hesitating. My eyes swivel left, unwillingly looking for the pregnancy tests. I grab a couple of them, hurrying to the register. I bury them at the bottom of my pile of purchases, going red as the bored-looking cashier scans them.

Once I'm at home, I stash the pregnancy tests under the bathroom sink, all the way in the back under the cleaning supplies. I tell myself that I don't need to take a test if I get my period in the next few days.

Two hours later though, I am back in the bathroom, pulling one of the tests out. I flip to the back of the box, reading the instructions. They're pretty basic.

Urinate on the test stick. Wait two minutes. Check for a plus sign or a minus sign on said stick.

I lean against the bathroom vanity and stare at the

test, telling myself it will be okay. The test is going to be negative, and I will laugh about this later. And never, ever tell Monster.

I don't know what his reaction would be, exactly... but I know I'm definitely supposed to... I don't know... *prevent* these kinds of things from happening. In some way, or another, even though I don't exactly know which way would've been available to me before he let me come with him to New Orleans.

Then I get a flash of Monster's face when he eventually finds out that I'm pregnant. Because he would find out, and he would be pissed. Twisted with fury and black with rage, his imagined face scares me.

Biting my lip, I know I just need to take the damned test. I'm stringing myself along for some reason, drawing out my anticipation. I pee on the stick, waiting the whole painful two minutes. I rest the test on the vanity, and I sit on the edge of the toilet seat.

In my head, I'm already scolding myself for not having figured out birth control before now. I mean, I was definitely a virgin when Monster bought me... but still, I know some things.

I know that condoms are a thing. But trying to imagine Monster's face after I suggest using them doesn't really bode well. That leaves me with... what, the pill?

I can take a pill every day, I guess. It's better than the alternative, right?

Crap, it's been two minutes. I stand and look at the test. I see a little + sign and my heartbeat starts racing.

Pregnant.

It's not possible, not in the least.

My eyes start to mist over, even though I'm sure that the test is wrong. With shaking hands, I pull out a second test. I take it, pacing anxiously.

Thinking about how badly I will be beaten when I tell Monster my news. Even if I don't tell him today, he will figure it out eventually. It's one of those medical ailments that you can't really hide for long.

When the second test tells me the same thing as the first, I smash it to the floor, letting out a wail.

Pregnant.

How?

How could it be possible? I can only barely take care of myself. I'm not only worried about being too young, but I'm also anxious because I have so little control over my entire life. I know nothing about babies... and I've only just convinced Monster not to *kill* me.

What am I going to do now?

Sinking to the floor, I cover my face and sob.

17

ARSEN

I head up the elevator to the apartment, holding a couple of wine bottles under one arm. I'm in a good mood. One of the mid-level, Salvadorian dealers has been quite chatty while under duress. I'm hunting that piece of shit Arturo to the ground, burning every place he could be hiding.

I think within this week I'll have him in hand. That fact makes me smile.

It also makes me realize that I've been home very little this whole week. Which in turn make me homesick. Actually, it just makes me long for Fiore's touch.

The apartment itself, I could do without. It's just to please Fiore if I'm honest with myself.

And that is what I'm about to do... please Fiore, in a different way. I can imagine her breathy sighs of pleasure, as I nod to the guard at the front door.

Inside, I can't find her anywhere at first glance. It's only once I venture to put down the wine in the kitchen, that I spot her way out on the terrace, looking down at the street below. Frowning, I open the French doors.

She turns her face toward me, and I can tell that something is wrong. Her face is pink and puffy. It's cold out here, and she exhales a puff of breath as she wipes at her face.

"Come in here," I call to her. "It's too cold for you to be hanging around out here."

She shivers underneath her dark peacoat, obediently hustling inside. Once I shut the door after her, she goes to sit on the biggest couch in the living room without a word to me.

Eyebrows raised, I follow her. "What's wrong?"

She sits on a pile of chenille throws, pulling them onto her lap. Her eyes are on her lap, unreadable. She just shrugs one shoulder, wiping at her face again.

"Is this about your run in with Dryas?" I ask, sitting down beside her.

Her eyes jump up to meet mine, surprised. "Elian told you?"

I nod. "He did. What did my brother say that upset you so much?"

Her eyes jerk down again, her mouth pulling into a tight pucker. "Did Elian happen to tell you about how Dryas kissed me?"

My mouth creases into a frown. "He did, yes."

"Tell me again about how Dryas isn't a threat? How he showed up when you weren't around, offering money and passage if I would get out of town and not tell you where I was going."

This shocks me. "What? Did he say why?"

She plucks at the blankets in her lap, her brow drawing down. "Because you care for me. I don't factor into the future he has planned for you, I guess."

I try to think of what that could possibly mean. "I find that... odd."

"He said you called a meeting of the three brothers for later tonight. He said you were going to tell one of them to take over the city, and it is my fault."

I don't know what to say to that, exactly. I haven't told Fiore of how I feel about her. Dryas is right about what I plan on announcing tonight, though.

I just can't give New Orleans the attention it deserves, not with Fiore here. With her blonde hair and plump pink lips, she would prove too tempting a target, that's for sure. I would just be counting down the hours until she disappeared, her dead body delivered to me sometime later.

"Dryas was right when he said I called a meeting," I say carefully. "It's not anybody's fault, though."

She tilts her head to the side. "And the part about leaving New Orleans? Is that right?"

I nod slowly. "Yeah. He had to know that at the rate I was going, I want to be around for that long. I've been burning the candle at both ends for years. He had to have known that I wouldn't last much longer. I can't even say that I'm surprised that he guessed at what the meeting is about."

Her face, normally so expressive, is closed and shuttered. I wish like anything that she would look up at me, but I don't want to force her. Besides, there is plenty on my own mind and in my own eyes that I wouldn't want her to see.

I stand, stalking to the kitchen and opening a wine bottle. I pour myself a glass, nearly chugging it. I pour a second, drinking half of it in one gulp.

It's easier for me to blunt the edges with a little wine, than it is to sit with the truth for one goddamn minute. I don't want her to see it, either.

I wouldn't want her to see what a terrible man I am. How murderous I am. How I just take what I want and leave the rest to burn.

I wouldn't want her to know about my past either. How before her, I dated strictly prostitutes, women that I could pay for their company and silence.

And above all else, I wouldn't want her to know that I've completely fallen in love with her. I would do anything to prevent her from seeing me, really seeing to the depths of my soul like that.

The idea of being seen, being judged, being really truly being visible and naked to another human being like that... it *terrifies* me. Because, at the end of the day, I need her to look at me with some kind of respect, even if it's learned the wrong way.

I know, without a doubt, that if she looks at me any other way I will fail to live up to her imaginings.

When I turn from the kitchen island, Fiore is there. Watching me with those baby blue eyes. Threatening me without saying a fucking word.

Does she even know what she's doing to me right now? I would be that she doesn't.

"Have a glass of wine," I say, turning and grabbing a second glass.

She clears her throat, her voice weak. "No."

Cocking a brow, I turn to her. "What do you mean, no?"

She folds her arms across her chest, the movement clearly defensive. "I said no to the wine. What's the problem with that?"

I narrow my gaze.

"You usually don't say no to me." Pouring a little half glass, I slide it closer to her. "Indulge me on this."

She looks at it but doesn't take it. Squaring her jaw, she shakes her head. "I can't."

Then her eyes widen as if she's said too much. "I mean, I don't want it."

But it's too late. I can almost smell her deception, so desperate am I to change the subject.

"You said can't." I set my glass down hard, causing it to ring out loud in the echo-y space. "What did you mean by that?"

Fiore tosses her head, biting her lip. Her voice comes out all breathy. "Nothing."

"Nothing?" I round the kitchen island, stalking her mercilessly. "I think it's something more than that. What did you do, take a drug like Xanax? Huh? You're afraid the alcohol will interact with it?"

She looks pissed off, biting off her answer. "No."

For every step that I take forward, she backs up. We move in a slow dance as if we are the hunter and the hunted. "Trying to lose weight? Maybe you've learned how many calories are in wine or something, hmm?"

She hugs herself and scowls. "No."

I smile wickedly. "I don't think it's for religious reasons. Otherwise, there are a lot of things you would have to give up, and I don't think you'd like it."

She blushes. "I could be religious. You don't know."

"I would know by now," I tell her, reaching out and grabbing her by the waist. "You wouldn't have enjoyed half of our fucking so goddamn much, I assure you."

She squeals as I pull her closer. "Monster—"

I kiss her, taking her mouth with as much passion and dominance as I can muster. Bruising her lips, I drive my hands into her hair. When I pull away, she's breathing hard. Her breath fans my face, her eyes scanning my expression closely.

"I could make this much easier on you," I taunt. I know she's just being stubborn at this point, so I am too. I don't even care about whether or not she drinks. It's just a means to an end, at this point. "You just have to say yes to the wine."

"Monster, I can't," she insists softly. "I... I don't want to hurt the baby."

I actually let out a bark of laughter. Where did she get the idea that this would be a funny trick? "Yeah, right. What baby?"

I expect her face to crinkle with laughter, but she remains sober and serious. "I just found out last night. I'm pregnant."

I feel her shrink back as if to ward off a blow from me. And then I realize that she's entirely serious. She's carrying a child.

My child.

Not just that, but she's actually worried that I will beat her for it. I stare at her for a few seconds, the shock of her announcement making me freeze. Fiore twists, trying to get out of my grasp. I instinctively hold her tighter, watching the fear play out on her face.

"You're sure?" I say, trying to calm my racing pulse. There is a faint roaring in my ears, the sound far away.

Her eyes filling with tears, she bites her full bottom lip and nods. When she speaks, she flinches. Her voice is so low, it's barely there. "Pretty sure."

My grip on her eases. I look down at her flat stomach, still in shock. "A baby?"

I put my palm over her stomach as if I can somehow feel the life growing inside. I've never considered the concept of having a child with half of my DNA. A little boy with my dark hair, or maybe a little girl with Fiore's gorgeous blonde tresses?

A tear breaks away and tracks down Fiore's face. "Are you angry?"

I shake my head. "How can I be? I'm just... I've never considered that anyone would have my child."

Even saying it feels funny on my tongue. I cup her cheek, smoothing away the track her tear left behind with the pad of my thumb. Her eyes have never looked so blue before, her skin never so translucent. Even her lips look more pink than I thought possible, her hair blonder.

"You thought I would be angry? You thought I would lash out at you?" I wonder.

She swallows heavily. "Yes."

"I could never do that to you now. I... I can't say that

I'm a different person than I was a few months ago, but... I love you, Fiore."

She flinches again. Her responses are so unexpected. "You're just saying that because I'm pregnant."

I lean in and kiss her again, taking her lips with all the slow-simmering passion that has been building in me since I realized that I love her. She gasps, her lips parting. Inviting my tongue's invasion, she brings her hands up to burrow in my hair.

My tongue sweeps her mouth. I love the way she tastes, like honey and mint and just a hint of sweet vanilla. I love how responsive she is to my kiss, her fingers curling against the back of my scalp, breathing hard, her chest heaving. I dip her back a little and see how her eyes close, her eyelashes falling against her cheek.

"I love you, Fiore," I whisper when I can bear to break away. "I'll love anything you bring me, even if that means a child. I promise you that."

Her eyes open, tearful. "Are you sure? Because I can't stand the idea of somehow driving you away. I love you too, so much that it hurts."

My mouth kicks up. "I swear it."

She hugs me then, and I pick her up, carrying her backward toward the bedroom.

18

FIORE

Monster carries me backward into the bedroom, carefully dropping me onto the bed. I look at up him, at his tall, suited form. I want him naked, on top of me, driving into me. I want him to lick my pussy, to tease my clit until I call out his name and drive my nails into my back. I want him to grab my hair, to flip me over, to take me from behind, sinking into me in that brutal way that I crave.

I fucking want him, so much. Over and over, in every conceivable way. I think that I will always want him this badly. At least, I hope so.

I blush and bite my lip when I realize that I'm already getting wet.

He does this to me.

"Like what you see, princess?" he growls.

Monster reaches a hand down to my face, brushing my hair from my eyes. He tucks it gently behind my ear, fixating me with his piercingly grey eyes. Then he chuckles.

"It's okay to look. I like you looking at me. I like *seeing* you looking at me more."

"Even then, it's rude to stare." I avert my gaze and focus on my knee instead.

"Princess, you can stare at me all you want. As long as it's me you're staring at like that, I'm happy. Fucking ecstatic, actually." He cups my chin so that our eyes meet. He holds my gaze, still not moving to hide any part of himself.

I start tracing the lines of his chest, then the ones of his arm, all the way to his hand. Next, I trace the muscular lines of his stomach down to his hips.

His breath hitches, and his cock twitches. I bite my lip, and he lets out a low moan.

"I'm really trying to let you do your thing here, princess. But you're really fucking killing me."

I grin at his words. A shiver of excitement runs up my spine and I can feel myself growing wet already.

"Fuck," he breathes as I run my hands over the outline of his hard cock over his briefs. "I can't fucking wait to get inside of you."

He flips me onto my back and presses his body to mine, kissing me deeply. He traces the neckline of my tank top as he runs his other hand up and down my thigh.

I moan as he reaches for the hem of my shirt, but I am surprised; instead of my shirt, he starts pulling off my yoga pants. I help him, and the second he has gotten them off, he's like a kid in a candy store.

He runs his hands up and down my smooth legs, looking at them like they are something delicious to be eaten. The look makes the fine hair on my neck rise. I'm glad that I know him because if a stranger looked at me with that kind of naked lust in his eyes, I would be afraid.

With Monster, though, fear has become... not impossible, but unlikely. I don't feel it when he looks at me, or when he kisses me. I certainly don't feel afraid when he holds me close. I shut my eyes for a second, nearly overcome with sensation and emotion at once.

"Fiore," he says softly. "Look into my eyes for a second."

I open my eyes and he drinks me in. He spends a minute running one hand up and down my side, leaving goosebumps trailing along my skin. He teases my nipples through my shirt, planting soft kisses on the exposed skin of my stomach.

I barely manage a nod. My skin is on fire everywhere he touches me, aching for more. Each stroke on my nipples causes my pussy to clench.

I am pretty sure that by now, my panties are drenched. I would be embarrassed if I could bring myself to think that far. But all my thoughts are completely focused on what he is making me feel.

His hands slide my panties down, and my tank top disappears over my head. If this were anyone else, I would be trying to cover up, but I force myself not to. The way he is looking at my body, his eyes dark with lust, make me feel hot and naughty.

He does this to me.

He drinks me in with his eyes, growling softly as his fingers stroke my dripping slit.

"God, Fiore. You're so fucking wet."

He brings his glistening fingers to his lips, licking my juices off the tips of his fingers. He closes his eyes and lets out a low moan as he tastes me on his hands. "Fucking delicious, princess. So sweet. I can't fucking wait to taste more."

I focused on his fingers that are once more playing with my clit, teasing the seam of my pussy.

He kisses me deeply, hungrily. I could feel his rock-hard cock digging into my soft belly. I moan loudly, still unable to form any words.

"Fuck, Fiore. I've never come from just sounds before, but if you keep that up, that might change." His voice was husky, low.

"Yes, please Monster! Please!" I beg.

I barely register that I haven't showered yet before his mouth is licking slowly but hungrily along my seam. Up and down, sucking in my lips, darting his tongue into me before starting all over again. He lets out a low moan again.

"So fucking sweet, Fiore." He moans before taking my sensitive clit in his mouth, sucking lightly, his tongue flicking against my bud.

It's a little like being struck by lightning, that first touch of his tongue to my clit. His tongue is turning me into a shivering, moaning maniac.

I try to buck my hips against him, unable to contain myself any longer, but his strong hands on my hips keeps me in place. He licks and sucks until I see nothing but stars and fireworks, feeling like I am about to fly away if it wasn't for him anchoring me.

Far too soon, the pressure that had been building up

inside me releases into a ball of light. My mind shatters in every different direction possible as I scream his name, digging my fingers into his shoulders and tugging at his hair.

He keeps licking, although he is very gentle now, aware of how sensitive I must be. I have to pull him away, and he comes up looking immensely self-impressed.

"Enjoy that, did you, princess?" he says, licking at his mouth.

"You know I did." I tug him close for a kiss and taste my own juices, sharp and sweet.

He takes his shirt off and pushes his pants down his legs. He moves to lie between my legs, our embrace one of comfort, of two people who know one another. I can feel the blunt tip of his cock against my entrance, positioned perfectly to slide into my pussy. He doesn't though.

He just kisses me hard. I can still taste myself on his lips. Somehow, it just arouses me even more. I moan into his mouth and hear a low sound at the back of his throat.

"You want it?" he says, so low it's almost a whisper. "Tell me how badly you want my cock, little girl."

"You know I do," I whisper, writhing.

He moves a little, shifts very slightly, and I can feel the promise of his weight, his body heat. I shiver.

"Are you sure?" he asks, teasing now.

"I want you inside of me. Now! Please, Monster."

He lets out a low growl but doesn't say any more. I can feel his hard cock gently pushing harder at my entrance. He slides in slowly, watching my every facial expression, seemingly gauging my every move.

"Fuck, you're so tight," he breathes as he stretches me inch by inch.

Pleasure fills my body, taking over every inch of me. The entire world disappears. All that exists is the feeling of his cock in me, his body on mine, breathing deeply and softly, growling and moaning into my ears. He kisses me and whispers to me.

"Fuck, you feel so good, Fiore."

He rocks into me with perfect rhythm, with just the right amount of pressure. I can feel my body begin to tighten, to draw taut like a bowstring.

It is so good, yet almost painful at this point. I feel so delightfully used, feel stretched out by his massive cock. I know he isn't going to stop, but that doesn't keep me from encouraging him.

"Don't stop, Monster. I'm so close," I urge. "I'm right there. Make me come."

I know he can. I will him to release the tension building in my breasts, in my core. His breathing is ragged now. I can feel his muscles starting to shake as he thrusts into me more forcefully, but he is still taking care not to hurt me. He is nearly there, and I am right there with him.

A final thrust and my world shatters into a million pieces again. The knot that has been building inside me releases.

He nips at my bottom lip, then his eyes roll back, his muscular shoulders flexing, his thighs shaking as he fills me to the brim. I feel his orgasm pour into my core, his cock twitching deep inside of me.

And it is the most exquisite thing.

For long minutes afterward, I lie there, clinging to his sweat-dampened body. I swear I can feel his heart racing in time with my own as we both suck in long, deep breaths. After a while, he shifts his weight off of me, pulling me close as he stretches out on the bed.

I raise my hand to push my hair back from my forehead and catch him looking at me. Not sexually, not angrily. Not with that expression of distance he used to get right before he got up to leave me alone for the rest of the night.

This time he looks at me... fondly. With an expression of tenderness.

"Do you know how fucking much I love you?" he says, his voice hoarse.

My cheeks turn pink. "Monster—"

"Arsen," he corrects me gently. His lips twitch. "You realize that you'll have to stop calling me Monster in public? Now that you're carrying my child, we wouldn't want people to get the wrong idea about us."

I laugh. "It would be unseemly."

He pauses, obviously trying to decide how to say something. "How do you feel about... you know..."

I raise an eyebrow. "About being pregnant?"

"Yes. About that."

"I don't know. I mean, I was so worried about what you would think, how mad you would be..." He flinches at my words, and I put a staying hand on his arm. "It is what it is. I really haven't had time to think about it. I mean... I'm young..." I pause, biting my lip. "But I'm also in love with you. And I know that I'm carrying your baby. That part, I'm definitely okay with."

He nods quietly. "Can you imagine, a baby that is half mine and half yours?"

I smile. "It'll be so damn gorgeous. That baby will be breaking hearts before it's out of middle school."

"Actually... you didn't go to middle school, did you?"

I shake my head. "Nope. After my mother passed away, I was homeschooled. For whatever that is worth, I guess."

"I didn't go to school, either. My brothers and I were too busy trying to keep ourselves off the streets."

I put my head down, all but pressing my face into his chest. "This baby will know privilege, then. It's already going to be better off than either of us, isn't it?"

When he responds, his voice rumbles up from his chest. "Yes. It will be taken care of."

"And loved," I whisper, my eyes growing heavy.

"Definitely that." He throws his arm over my body, and I drift off to sleep.

19

ARSEN

$\mathcal{I}$ climb the stairs of the little balcony that Dryas has picked as our meeting place. Each step is heavy, each footfall one closer to the moment when I tell my brothers what I have planned.

I know that my brothers will be angry at my announcement. I know I was meant to do better. Meant to be better at taking over New Orleans. After all, it is what I've single-mindedly worked toward for two years.

But then I picture Fiore's delicate frame, her face smiling, and I just can't take the chance. Because the ruler of New Orleans needs to be cruel and hard... and most importantly, he can't have anything worth losing.

If my enemies knew anything about Fiore, or if they figured out that she's pregnant... she would be snatched off the street so fast, it's not even funny. I'd give up anything to get her back, even though anyone smart would make sure I never saw her again.

I just know that I can't live like that, wondering if

Fiore is okay, wondering when she'll be taken from me. I won't.

Reaching the top of the stairs, I see with some surprise that Dryas is waiting, drink in his hand. He turns, his lips lifting as he sees me. He lifts his glass to me.

"Brother," he says, greeting me simply.

I glance around the balcony, which has a few tables. I stroll onto the floor, but inside I am a tangle of knots. It's not like me to be nervous about things like this. "Where is Damen?"

He shrugs his suit-clad shoulders. "Does it matter? We both know that we are the brains of the operation, while Damen is the terrifying hound we keep chained up until we need him."

I sigh, looking around for a waiter. I would like a drink, too. To calm my fucking nerves. Honestly, Dryas isn't wrong about Damen, but I had hoped to have him here to take my side. After all, it was Damen that got all mystical and encouraged me to find my High Priestess, whatever the fuck that means.

The waiter comes up the same set of stairs.

"Thank God," I say. "A Vieux Carré for me."

Dryas wanders over to the edge of the balcony, looking down as he takes a drink from the glass in his hand. "Do you know that they grease the poles under the balconies here during Mardi Gras? It's supposed to be to keep the hoi polloi from drunkenly climbing up the poles and looting in the hotels. Of course, being New Orleans, it turns into a circus. They have a party and drink more to celebrate the greasing of the poles."

I take a seat underneath a bright red patio umbrella. I'm not sure what Dryas is even talking about. "You don't say."

He turns to me with a humorless smile. "There are tons of those odd traditions here, in a city that is as old as this one. Did you know that New Orleans is almost three hundred years old?"

I look at my watch. Is Damen not coming or is he just late? Dryas didn't say either way. "Is there a reason you are so full of trivia right now, Dryas?"

He sits down across the table from me. "What else are we supposed to do to pass the time? Not all of us can devote months of our lives to training a whore to do everything we like, can we now? It would be insane."

Ah, there it is. Dryas is obsessing about Fiore, making her the centerpiece of his troubles. In truth, it is me that is failing him, or maybe his own ambitions. Either way, blaming her will not help him, and I think part of him knows it.

The waiter returns just as I am considering my brother through slitted eyes. He sets my drink down and scurries down the stairs once more.

"You've been stalking her," I say idly, picking up my drink. I take a sip, feel the burn traveling down my throat.

He smirks. "Can you really stalk a slave? Stalking is to strike fear into someone by following them. And slaves don't have feelings, from what I have heard."

I actually growl at that. "Stop calling her a slave."

"What?" he taunts. "She's so much more than that? You've given her your heart?"

He laughs at that, the timbre of his voice deep and haunting.

I set my glass down, my mood turning black. "And what would you know about it? I seem to remember that the only girl you ever loved died horribly. She burned to death, didn't she?"

Dryas lurches to his feet, swearing. "I'll fucking kill you."

"I'd like to see you try." I stand up, a reminder that we can go toe to toe. We are perfectly matched, except for one thing...

I have something to fight for. A face to keep in the back of my mind.

Dryas doesn't.

"Will you two calm the fuck down?" I turn to see Damen at the top of the stairs, looking at the two of us like we're insane. "Don't you think that our rivals want the two of you at each other's throats like this?"

Dryas folds his arms across his chest. "You're one to talk. Last I heard, you had run off with some girl too. Where is she, waiting for you in the car like a gun moll?"

Damen levels a look at Dryas. "Why are you suddenly so bitter?"

"Ask Arsen. Arsen, why am I so bitter? Why now? Could it be that I don't want to lose hold of a city we've worked for years to take hold of?"

Damen and Dryas both stare at me. In the pit of my stomach, acid burns. "Fiore's pregnant. I can't risk her life and the baby's life, not after what happened to Anna. Would you want to look forward to the day when you open a box and find Bianka's head, Damen?"

Damen pales a little. "No, of course not."

Dryas makes a strangled noise. "I'm surrounded by the worst kind of fools. Men in love will do anything that will turn their beloved's head."

I growl again. "I'm not trying to turn Fiore's head, I'm trying to keep it attached to her body. And close to me, I suppose."

"Wait, wait. So, you've made your announcement?" Damen interrupts me.

I cross my arms. "No. Dryas is jumping the gun, as usual."

Dryas sneers at me, which makes my lips turn up.

"Go ahead, then. Make your announcement," he grits out.

Looking back and forth between my two brothers, I sigh. "I plan to step down as the public face of the Cypriot faction in the takeover of New Orleans. It's really not a choice; I have to. I have a couple of plans ready to drop into place."

"Really?" Damen asks, looking intrigued.

"Fucking asshole," Dyas spits out. "It looks like he's chained to that good pussy he's been getting. What do Americans say, pussy whipped?"

I grimace. "You're just angry because she turned down your proposals. Did you know that, Damen? He tried to buy Fiore's attentions and he was rejected."

"I'm not trying to get revenge. I'm trying to keep what we've worked toward for so long!" Dryas roars.

"Calm the fuck down," Damen says. "And stop intentionally making him angry, Arsen. For the love of God, it's not good when I'm the most sane one of the three of us."

Dryas and I quiet down, glaring at each other. Damen points at me, his brow furrowed. "You said you have backup plans. What are they?"

I suck in a breath and force myself to even out before responding. "There are options. One of you can take the reins, which would be preferable. At least until this period of bloodshed is over. Or, we can set a puppet as figurehead here, someone malleable. We have plenty of underlings to choose from."

Dryas looks contemptuous. "One of us can step in and take care of things during the hard parts, you mean."

I look at Damen. "I would suggest you because you're not visibly insane."

Damen ignores me. "A puppet would be tolerable, but we have no guarantee that he will hand the business back to us when we're ready. I don't know if I'm willing to risk that."

"Why would we hand the business off to someone else?" Dryas raves. "That would be suicide. We might as well just vacate the city! Why the fuck have we done any of this, huh? Was it to make it this far, only to give up because one of us wants to start a family?"

I grit my teeth. "We never discussed what we would do in this scenario. I never imagined it. Honestly, it is just as surprising to me as it is to anyone else involved."

Dryas leans in. "Maybe I should solve the problem myself. Fiore is clouding your judgment. She has been, ever since the first time I laid eyes on you two together. It would be better if I just made her disappear."

For a second, I say nothing. I can only hear the blood rushing in my head. Everything is tinged red, just like the first time I killed someone out of anger. I take one breath, then another.

Dryas just threatened Fiore. Not just that, he just threatened the family I can *barely* claim to have. He talks about Fiore like she isn't the only bright star in the deep black sky of my anger and hatred and rage.

"Arsen," I hear Damen say, coming over to put his hand on my shoulder.

For some reason, that touch is the trigger. And I am the bullet, shooting my whole body out across the table toward Dryas. The table starts to tip as Dryas comes back at me, bucking.

"What?" he snarls. "I said it. I should kill your girl, hands down. She's in the way of plans we've worked to complete for *years*."

I grab the edge of the table and turn it over to the side, where it crashes against the building. Both of our glasses fall to the ground, smashed beyond reckoning. "You fucking coward. I can't believe you would be so stupid. If New Orleans is so important, then *you* stay and defend it."

He circles, forcing me to move. Soon we are both circling each other, our fists in the air, ready to attack.

"You think I don't want to?" he grunts. "I have other things to do than to clean up your messes, little boy."

"What, like go after Father Derrick some more? When will you get it through your head that the girl you loved is gone?" I let out a bewildered laugh, shaking my head. "The Brotherhood, or whatever the fuck they're calling themselves these days... they found out about you two, and..."

I draw a finger across my neck, making a cutting sound.

"Arsen," Damen warns.

Dryas scoops up one of the pieces of broken glass on the floor, his face contorting with rage. He launches himself at me with a primal scream, knocking Damen to the side.

I'm ready for him, grabbing his hands as we both topple over to the ground. Dryas is wild-eyed, his breathing erratic. He lands on top of me, trying to stab me with the shard of broken glass. I grab his hands, closing them a little.

The glass cuts into his hand, but he doesn't even wince. Blood pours from his hand onto my chest and face. I can taste his blood in my mouth as I grimace and try harder to close his hand around the shard, to force his hand away from my body.

Damen groans angrily and tries to tackle Dryas off of me. In the moment of confusion, I let Dryas go. That's all the time Dryas needs to turn the glass shard outward and plunge it into my ribs.

I open my mouth as a bright blossom of pain sprouts up on my side. Looking down at my wound, I see Dryas is grinding the shard against his own sticky red fingers, driving it as deep as it will go.

"This is what I will do to your girl," he whispers brusquely, flecks of spit flying out of his mouth to hit my face. "Then you'll wish you'd thought twice when you had the chance to save Aurelia. You will *pay* for that, brother."

"Dryas, what the *fuck*?" Damen yells, prying Dryas off of me.

I look down again and see blood pumping from my wound. The fucker didn't just stab me, he must have hit an artery too.

Dryas just stands up, limping a little, and grins. "You're going to die, right here, right now. Then we'll see who the best of the three of us really is."

"Get the fuck out of here!" Damen cries, falling to his knees beside me. "Oh shit. He got you bad, Arsen..."

"Fuck. You." I manage to heave out the words as I fall onto my back.

As I lie there, pumping blood onto the ground, I grab for Damen.

"Fiore... you have to..." I suck in a breath, wheezing. "You have to take care of..."

And then everything is black.

20

FIORE

*N*o.

It can't be true.

Monster... Arsen... he can't be dead.

When Jack tells me, my mouth flies open, the steaming mug of tea falling to the floor and shattering all around me like so much noise. One hand flies to my abdomen, unconsciously protecting the faint flicker of life within.

"Ma'am?" Jack says. "Ma'am, should we go to the hospital?"

He's looking at me for instructions. I clutch the counter to keep myself from falling. "What... what did the doctor say?"

He gives his head a little shake. "I don't know, ma'am. It was Damen that called, saying he was on his way to Tulane Hospital. He only had a second to use the phone."

"And... he didn't say what happened to Arsen?" I ask, my chin wobbling.

"No, ma'am. He just said to come as fast as you can." His brow wrinkles with concern.

The only thing is, I'm not even a hundred percent sure that this isn't some kind of setup. If someone was trying to get me to leave my house and rush somewhere, this would be the way to do it.

"Hold on," I say, holding a finger up. "Let me try his cell."

I call Monster's cell number, my heart pounding. I grab my cell phone from where I left it on the bed, pressing it close to my ear. Each ring seems to take forever. Finally, his voicemail picks up, something that hasn't happened the whole time that we've been together.

My whole face collapses. I try to stave off tears as I look around. "Fuck! Let me get my coat. We'll go right now."

As I pull my coat from the coat rack beside the front door, I can't stop picturing Monster — Arsen, I correct myself — dying. For some reason, I imagine Arsen in the place of my mother, dead in that little bed in that god-awful dark basement.

I repress a sob. It seems like an eternity for the elevator to come up. Shuffling inside with all three of the guards assigned to me, I'm certain that we're in some kind of Kafka-esque nightmare, the clock in my head counting down the seconds until...

What? They pronounce him dead?

I place my hand against my stomach as the guards drive me over to the hospital. Every red light is a torment, every bit of traffic sheer torture. I'm on high alert as we head to the hospital, expecting something to happen at any moment.

An explosion that rocks the car.

Gunfire that riddles us with bullets.

A freaking surface-to-air missile, for God's sake.

Anything that would mean I was wrong, that someone wanted to lure me out of the apartment, that Arsen is safe. I would trade myself for him, at this moment. But I don't know about our baby...

I am going to have to get used to thinking that whatever happens to me, happens to the baby too.

But nothing impedes our progress as we hurry to Tulane Hospital. I grip my comfortable grey sweatpants, realizing only then that I'm sort of half-dressed. Sweatpants, pink crop top, and a huge mint green winter coat over all that.

Well, I definitely look like I left in a hurry. When we pull up to the Tulane ER, Jack and I get out, sprinting inside the cool, white-tiled waiting room. I run right up to the reception desk, a little out of breath when I talk to a young male nurse.

"Arsen Aetós," I breathe onto the glass. "He's here, isn't he?"

The nurse narrows his eyes at me. "Are you family?"

"Yes. Wife! I'm his wife," I blurt out. Lying has lost its meaning here and now. The truth won't stand between me and Arsen, not if he's only lying a few dozen feet away.

The nurse clicks a few keys on the computer in front of him, then sighs. "He is here. He's in critical condition... the doctors are still working on him."

"What happened?" I ask, my voice cracking. "Is he going to be okay?"

Please, let him be okay.

The nurse's forehead wrinkles. "I'm not qualified to say, hon. Have a seat over there, and when one of his doctors asks for you, I'll let you know."

I start to cry. "Shit. Oh, God. Okay."

Jack puts his arm around me, steering me away from the reception desk. A door opens, and Damen comes out. He's covered in blood and looking grimly determined. When he sees me, I have the distinct impression that he is sorry.

"You're here," he sighs. "The doctors ran me out of there. They were busy taking his shirt off and trying to see where he was hurt."

Despite his expression, I still shrunk back into Jack's arms. "What happened?"

"What happened? Your stupid boyfriend talked shit to..." He drops his voice to a whisper. "Our brother... And he got himself stabbed."

"Dryas *stabbed* him?" I cry, drawing the attention of everyone in the room, including the nurse.

"Shhhh," Damen says, glancing around. "Yes. But if anybody asks, he was stabbed by a stranger."

"Why the fuck would I lie for Dryas?" I say, disbelieving.

Damen looks around again, clearly annoyed. He reaches out and grabs my wrist, trying to draw me toward the door. I violently shake him off, my jaw squaring.

"Don't touch me!" I hiss. "I'm not going outside, so you might as well say whatever you have to say here."

"Alright, alright. For fuck's sake, I should have brought Bianka." He rolls his eyes. "When Arsen wakes up—"

I fold my arms across my chest. "If. You mean *if* Arsen wakes up, don't you?"

Damen makes an aggravated noise. "When Arsen wakes up, he won't want the cops sniffing around our business. If you name the person that stabbed him, they'll be more interested than they have any right to be."

"I don't care about that!" I snap.

Damen gives me a look. "No, of course, you don't. How could Arsen have actually picked a girl that cares what happens to the family? It would go against the grain of who he is."

An alarm goes off behind the door that Damen came from, the emergency room. I faintly hear an automated voice. "Code blue, room E13. Code blue, room E13."

"Shit. That's the room that Arsen is in," Damen says, glancing up. "Excuse me? Excuse me, nurse? I'm going to need you to let me back in there. That code blue is my brother."

The nurse glances behind himself, then presses the buzzer. "Stay out of the doctors' way, okay?"

Damen and I are in lockstep as we race through the doorway and down the hall. He stops short, drawing my attention to a room filled with nurses and doctors. The room is separated from us only by a giant wall of glass. All of the medical staff are in motion, all attending to one person.

When one nurse moves out of the way, I can see Arsen, his face turned my direction. He looks pale, his eyes closed as one doctor tries to give him chest compressions. Everywhere I look, there are doctors and nurses touching his body, putting in IVs, propping his feet up for circulation.

"Code blue, room E13," the eerie voice says. "Code blue, room E13."

I see one doctor shaking her head, looking up at the large clock on the wall.

"No," I whisper to myself. I move forward, my palm coming up to graze the glass window between me and the whirlwind inside. "Keep going. Keep going!"

Damen stands beside me, watching anxiously.

Slowly, the doctors and nurses stop working, backing off. They are all looking either at the only doctor still performing chest compressions or at the big wall clock. One of the nurses touches the doctor's back, and she slows.

"It's time," the nurse says kindly.

"No!" I shout, banging on the glass. All the medical workers look up, frightened by the suddenness of my gesture.

"Can you go talk to them?" a nurse says to a doctor.

As I look on and bang on the glass wall, horrified, the doctor who was doing chest compressions calls out, "Time of death is 6:15 p.m."

"No! No, I just found him!" I scream. I'm sobbing openly now, tears streaming down my cheeks unchecked. "No, you have to save him! You have to try—"

Jack's big paw descends on me, dragging me back, away from Arsen. My stomach cramps suddenly and I hiss, drawing in on myself.

"Oh fuck! Oh! Oh, fuck! It hurts—"

Suddenly, I'm swarmed by doctors and nurses, the same people who were just moments earlier trying to save Arsen. The questions start.

"Are you okay? What hurts? Get a wheelchair..."

I collapse into the wheelchair, not even able to answer their questions beyond the fact that I am pregnant and yes, I think something is very wrong inside my stomach. I'm sobbing too hard, thinking of how Arsen and my mother looked exactly the same as they died.

I refuse to believe it.

No.

I won't believe it.

He can't be dead. He can't be... just gone.

I hugged him just this afternoon. I kissed him, cherished him, only hours ago.

What happened?

Eventually, I am given an oral sedative. An oxygen mask is forced on me, and I'm checked into the ER. I'm forced to lie on a gurney, to take slow breaths.

Do they not realize that my — what would I call Arsen... my everything? Did they not realize that I just lost my everything?

The sedative makes me woozy and calm... but it's a little like someone pressed MUTE on my emotions. They're still there, they are just much quieter than before. I lie there on the hospital bed, tears tracking down my face.

How could this have happened? It seems surreal.

I notice that Damen has disappeared. That's more than fine with me. Jack sticks close to me, staying me by side the whole time. Even when I am given a cup and told to pee in it, he holds the door open, shielding me from intrusive eyes.

I sleep a little, although if you'd offered it to me, I'd have turned it down. When I wake up, the whole staff has changed. The hospital is humming along as if Arsen never died just hours ago in the very next room.

I cry again, curling in on myself, great gasping sobs. My cramps are gone. But so, too, is Arsen.

What direction is my life taking, if it will no longer be shaped by such a strong and sure man? I press my hands against my abdomen, uncertain. I'm afraid for myself, and for my unborn child.

By the time I stumble out of the ER, with Jack putting my coat over my shoulders, I feel like someone has hollowed me out with a spoon and left me to dry out and blow away.

"Where would you like to go, ma'am?" Jack asks.

"Back to the apartment," I answer, my voice reed-thin. Because that is the last place that I was with him... and the only place that he left for me.

I stare out the window, hurting so much that I'm almost numb, and try not to think at all.

21

FIORE

I wake up in our bed, warm and safe. I remember things in a jumble; a story I want to tell Monster, the fact that I am pregnant, that we probably need some more coffee beans. I stretch, the tee shirt that I'm wearing without anything underneath sliding up my body.

Smiling, I know exactly who I should present my naked ass to, with the awareness that cupping and fondling will be forthcoming. Rolling over onto my side, I face Monster.

Only he's not there. An empty space greets me starkly, his side of the bed still made up.

That's when I realize that Monster *died* yesterday.

I sob out a breath, my heart hurting so damn bad I don't know to do with myself. It's a physical ache as much as it is a psychic one. I lie in our bed, crying out all the tears that I have to cry just now.

He's never going to touch me again. I'm never again going to lie in his arms, feeling safe and cared for.

I'm alone and lost, somewhere deep in my own ocean of grief. I know that there are other people who probably care about Arsen Aetós, but I still feel the solitude very sharply.

I'm without a companion or lover, forever.

The magnitude of that statement, the permanence of it, shakes me to my core. I wallow in it for a while, crying and watching the sun ascend to its place high in the sky, then begin to drop again.

In the afternoon, I have to get up. I have to pee. I'm desperately thirsty, drinking water right from the water pitcher in the fridge with the door open. I know I should eat something, if not for me then for the baby, but...

I just can't.

I settle on making some tea instead. While the water boils, I set up my tea bag and get the jar of honey out of the pantry. I discover that having my hands busy is a blessing of sorts; while I'm pouring the water and steeping the tea bag, I can only focus on that.

It doesn't lessen the loss or blunt the feelings. But it makes it bearable for those few minutes, those precious minutes while the tea sits. I stir in a spoonful of honey and sip the tea cautiously. It's a taste of sweet and mellow, reflecting sleepy jasmine and the sharp note of green tea.

It needs a little milk, I decide. Still holding the cup, I open the refrigerator. I pour a little bit of milk in my cup, swinging the door closed again.

And then I drop the cup, staring at the man right in front of me. Tall, dark, handsome as sin. The teacup shatters everywhere, instantly forgotten.

"Monster?" I whisper, putting my hand to my throat.

Am I seeing things?

But no, Monster steps toward me, his expression guarded. "Hello, Fiore."

My thoughts are a mess. I gape at him. "You... but you... I saw you..."

I take a step closer, wincing at the porcelain shards underfoot. I need to touch him, to see if he's real. I reach out and touch the solid flesh of his chest. Looking up at him with wonderment, I realize I've started to cry again.

"You're real?" I ask, perplexed.

"I am," he rumbles. Glancing down at my feet, he frowns. "Let's talk somewhere else."

He sweeps me up in his arms, though I'm still dumbfounded. How is this possible?

I saw his last moments.

I saw the doctor declare his time of death.

I watched as he *died*.

He carries me to the living room, setting me on the couch.

I grab his shirt, pulling him in for a kiss. A kiss, the simple gesture of love that an hour ago I never thought I would get again. My tears flow, and I simply let them.

He takes control of the kiss, his tongue rolling against mine, sweeping my mouth mercilessly. I mewl into his mouth, feeling pathetically happy. I'm so weak for this man, beyond needy. I want him... I need him.

I grip him, my movements frantic. I also have so many unanswered questions.

Why? How? I need answers. Pulling back, I wipe away my tears, and then I slap him right in the face.

Though he clearly wasn't expecting the slap, he doesn't move to retaliate either.

As Monster perches on the couch on his knees, he winces, moving a little stiffly. I sniffle, wiping at my eyes.

"How? How did you... what, fake your death?" I ask, growing more agitated. "And why?"

Monster purses his lips, taking a seat next to me. He examines my feet, wiping away spilled tea and a little blood. Again, he winces, reaching for his ribs. It's clear to me that he's been wounded there, so at least him getting stabbed was real.

"When Damen and I were in the ambulance, he whispered that if I wanted out, this was our chance. I realized he was right. The doctors and nurses that attended me pulled the glass from my wound and stitched me up. Then..." He looks down, showing the first sign of shame I've ever seen him display. "Damen went to tell you. You had to think it was real, so other people would believe it."

"Who? Who was watching?" I ask, frustrated.

"All of New Orleans was watching. And the people that need to be convinced that I'm dead, the people that would hurt you, they are currently holed up, trying to figure out their next move."

That doesn't make me feel a single bit less used. "I could kill you myself right now. I ought to. Did you know that I was hospitalized for a while yesterday, on account of having terrible cramps? I thought I was losing the baby!"

I slap his arm to punctuate my words. He looks pained.

"I'm sorry. If there was any other way to keep you safe..."

"You could've hurt our child!" I say, my brow drawing down. "You should've told me."

"There was no time," he insists, catching my hands in his. "It's not like I planned for Dryas to stab me."

I resist, still angry beyond explanation. "What would you have done if you had come back, only to find out that grief caused me to lose the baby, huh?"

He releases one of my hands, spreading his hand over my stomach. He looks at me, his grey eyes guileless. "I would've mourned. We would've mourned, together. But we are lucky, so we don't have to." He pauses, then arches his eyebrow. "Right?"

I stare at him for a few more seconds, then exhale slowly. The warmth from his palm is slowly sinking into my skin. I may be so mad at him that I can't think straight, but there is no denying that I love it. I love *him*. "Yes. We were lucky."

"And we don't have to worry about New Orleans. Damen has agreed to oversee the rest of the takeover until we agree that I ought to return."

Tossing my head, I am indifferent about that fact. "I don't care. I only care about you, and about the baby. I need you both to be okay. I need you both in my life. You hear me?"

Monster — Arsen, I remind myself — leans in to embrace me. And I let him.

More than that, I cling to him, my tears dampening his shoulder through his shirt. He holds me close and pets my hair.

"Don't cry," he murmurs into my ear. "I can't stand to see those tears and know they're because of me."

I raise my head, seeking out his mouth, and press mine against his. He kisses me passionately, making my senses tingle. I bury my fingers in his hair, breathing him in and kissing him at the same time.

He's okay.

My Monster is really okay.

I'm not alone after all. And soon, in just half a year, I will have a new life to hold close. A new soul that Arsen and I will bring into this world, together.

The kiss grows hot, and I pull back, breathing hard. I look at Arsen.

"Take me to the bedroom," I demand. "Show me how much you missed me."

He grins wickedly and presses his lips to mine, lifting me up in his arms.

22

FIORE
SIX MONTHS LATER

*E*arly in the morning, I wake with a groan. I have to pee again, which is unsurprising since the little girl in my womb has been awake all night and it feels like she's pressing right on my bladder. Flipping back the covers, I lever my pregnant body out of bed, getting up with difficulty.

Dressed in a flowing ivory caftan that Arsen hates, I pad to the bathroom. I pee like a racehorse, knowing already that this will only satisfy me for an hour. God, I loved being pregnant until I reached thirty-eight weeks.

But in the three weeks since then, I have come to view my pregnancy as being overly long and my little girl as being... not an unwelcome guest, but definitely one that is about to overstay her welcome. Swollen feet and hands, stretch marks, backaches...

And don't even get me started about the things I can't eat or take. Forget alcohol, no one told me that I can't eat unpasteurized cheeses or take a Tylenol. I can't wait until I'm not pregnant anymore. I have dreams about all the

French brie and hot dogs and NyQuil I'm going to put in my body, possibly all at once.

I'm not even going to talk about how excited I will be to wear my old dresses and jeans again. I might start to cry if I think about it for too long, which is another wonderful thing that no one told me about.

As I'm walking back to bed, though, my little girl kicks. My heart flutters, and I settle a hand on the shelf that the top of my belly has become. My lips twitch, and I know that excited as I am, I would not have missed out on this for the world.

When I climb back into bed, Arsen rolls over, looking at me sleepily. "You okay?"

I nod, turning my body around and presenting my butt to him. He groans, my ass managing to turn him on, though I'm personally disgusted by myself. He kneads the flesh of my ass, grinding his cock between my cheeks. I'm instantly wet, hormones flying all over the place.

I whimper, pulling one of his hands to my super sensitive breasts. His touch is gentle, pulling my caftan up and caressing my breasts lightly. I moan, already needy.

He pulls my caftan over my head and casts it aside. I sit up straight and reach up to him; he kisses me eagerly, nudging me back onto the bed. He kneels over me, his lips roaming to my neck, my collar bone, my exquisitely tender breasts.

"Ohh," I breathe, my fingers plucking at the tee shirt he fell asleep wearing.

I feel shy, my hands covering my huge baby bump, but he's having none of that. He grabs both of my hands, pinning them above my head, looking down at me.

"Do you even know how fucking hot you are?" he asks. He kisses my lips slowly. "I've wanted you so badly all day, Fiore."

Arsen releases my hands, his fingers toying with my pink nipples. He looks at me, maintaining eye contact as he takes a nipple in his mouth. I squirm; his tongue abrades my nipple and it feels so damn good.

He moves his lips from my nipple back up to my mouth. I growl with sudden impatience, pushing him to the side a little so I can get his shirt off. He pulls his shirt over his head with a grin, and I slide my hands down his legs to the boxer briefs he wears.

"Jesus," he says, his eyes fastened on my breasts. He reaches out with one hand and cups the heaviness of my breast. "Your tits have literally never looked better. They're so fucking perfect."

"You're wearing too many layers," I say, working on the last two buttons of his shirt.

He pauses for a second, then backs up, taking his boxers off. I've never been so glad to see my own boyfriend's cock as I am in the moment when he shoves his boxer briefs off.

Arsen stands there for a second, stroking his rock-hard cock, looking at me. And I stare right back at him; he's all lean flesh and muscle, looking hard and bearded. I'm not sure how I got so lucky, having such a man's man want *me*, but I don't question it.

"How are we going to do this?" he asks speculatively, looking at me. "I don't want to hurt the baby, with your due date so close."

"You won't," I promise. I bite my lip suggestively and

turn over, putting my ass in the air. It takes everything I've got to balance myself with my pregnant stomach, but he doesn't have to know that.

He growls and falls over me, stopping himself with an arm. He kisses the back of my neck and I shiver. Arsen's hands cup my hips, and he kisses me on the lower back.

"Mmmm," I sigh. He peels off my underwear, and then I'm bare before him.

Excitement skitters down my spine as his big hands shape my ass, and he reaches between my legs. I suck in a breath as he finds my clit with two fingers. It feels so incredibly good, I grind against his hand.

"You like that?" he says. I look back at him, blushing at the dirty tone of his voice.

"Yes," I say. "You know what would be better, though?"

He just grins and slips his two fingers into my pussy. "Fuckkkkk. You're so wet, princess."

"So, fuck me already," I say, pushing my ass back against his hand.

"If you say so."

Arsen withdraws, fisting his cock and positioning it near my entrance. He notches his head against my pussy, going very, very slowly. He only gets the head in before he starts to curse.

"Fuck," he says. "Goddamn, it's been too long since I had you."

"Oh, God," I moan, clutching the sheets. "I need you so badly. *Please*."

He slides home, filling me up all the way. I've never

been quite so full, but I feel that in the best way possible. I feel him hesitate, so I encourage him.

"Yes," I say as he withdraws and begins to plunge back in. "Right there, but *harder*."

He starts up a steady rhythm of thrusting and reaches around to my front. Arsen begins strumming my clit, which sends waves of sensation through my body. I start moaning, using one hand to tweak my own nipple.

"Fuck, princess," Arsen groans. "I'm not going to last long."

"Then do it harder," I whisper. "Fuck me like you mean it."

I try to zone out. It's not hard, between Arsen's thrusts and his clever fingers on my clit. I close my eyes and concentrate on the orgasm building inside me. With each thrust, I get closer until suddenly I shatter, screaming Arsen's name.

He comes just after me, his breathing ragged. I sag, losing the will to hold up my body any longer. We both melt into the mattress, boneless.

I lie there, trying to breathe. It's uncomfortable, being trapped between my own clumsy body and Arsen's more muscular one.

What am I thinking? Everything is uncomfortable these days. The idea of comfort is a fond memory.

Arsen gets up, kissing me on the lips. "Don't move."

Groaning a little, I flip myself over, scoping out Arsen's ass as he moves across the apartment. Damn, I know we just fucked, but that ass is making me horny all over again.

Not to mention when he comes back, I'll be able to ogle his cock. That thought makes me blush.

When he disappears from view, I lie back, looking up at the curtained windows. It's getting light out, which in itself is nice. One more day closer to having this baby in my arms... and off of my bladder.

Little... Willow? Or maybe Isabella? Amelia? Tabatha? Roxie? Lauren?

I run through the liturgy of names, still undecided. Theresa, for my mother? Trying to imagine a baby with that name though, I'm unconvinced.

Arsen returns, walking over to the bed with a big wooden tray. It's holding a small bouquet of flowers, a glass of orange juice, and a couple of slices of toast. He sets it down in front of me.

"For me?" I ask, raising my eyebrows.

His eyes sparkle as he winks at me. "It is Mother's Day, after all. I figure that applies to you."

Tears spring to my eyes. "Oh, Arsen. You didn't have to do that!"

"There's a little more," he says as I take a sip of the orange juice. Before I can say anything, he places a blue velvet ring box on the tray.

I sputter, putting the orange juice glass down on the tray. I wipe my mouth, looking up at him. "Arsen..."

"Open it," he says, cutting me off.

Tears begin to overwhelm me. I pick the ring box up. Arsen kneels as I open the box. I'm blubbering like a fool by the time that I take in the large, pristine diamond in its simple platinum setting.

"Fiore, once Katherine Carolla—" he starts.

I hiccup and sob, totally unable to control my emotions.

Luckily, he's placid enough. "I love you. I'm lucky enough to be in love with you. You're carrying my child. Will you do me the distinct honor of being my bride?"

Overwhelmed by emotion, I can only nod. When I can speak, I sob out, "Y-yes. I love you so m-much... it's unbelievable, Arsen."

He pulls me into his arms and kisses me. I'm safe and warm and loved.

And that's all I ever wanted.

Everything else is just another cherry on top of my sundae.

23

DRYAS

ST-MALO, FRANCE — A FEW MONTHS LATER

*S*taring out the the window onto the warm, lamplit street, I sip the rough whiskey that's in my tumbler. I can see the cobblestones, can make out the letters on the sign on the building opposite me, so it is not too late. It is maybe eight-thirty, no later.

I take another swig. It is rotgut stuff, making me wince as it burns its way down my throat. But it keeps the dreams of Arsen at bay late at night, and makes the days pass more quickly.

Unbidden, the image of my brother swims up to me. Arsen, just as he realizes that I have stabbed him. When he looks into my eyes for the last time.

When he knows that he will never see his slave girl again, or his child be born.

Shaking my head to clear the vision, I slam the rest of the whiskey down.

Since I killed my brother last year, I have tried to refocus my energies. He was right about one thing;

revenge has been in my heart ever since Aurelia died, bleeding to death alone in the street.

No longer will revenge be in my heart... no after I find the men responsible and slit their throats. Just for fun, I may drink their blood, too.

Bloodshed is my closest friend, these days.

I turn to the door of the little one-room apartment when I hear it begin to open. A man pokes his head in.

Thin and weasely, he darts a furtive look around around before his gaze settle on me. "Monsieur."

"Please tell me you've finally got him," I say, setting my cup aside on the mantle place. "Otherwise, you're not going to be paid for this little adventure all around the coast of France."

The man blanches. His English is very heavily accented, not unlike mine. "Oui, monsieur. We have got him in the very next room."

I narrow my eyes at him. "Are you sure? I don't want this one to end up not being the right man, after all. Remember, I only want to talk to the man who was dispatched to kill the girl."

The man bows. "Oui, yes. This is the men that says he worked for La Fraternité. The Brotherhood, I mean to say."

"And Father Derrik?" I ask, arching a brow.

"The man claims he worked directly for him. He says they worked... how do you say? Hand and hand? Into the hand?"

"Shut up," I tell him. "Let me get my tools, then I'll be right there."

"Monsieur," he says, disappearing.

I go over to my suitcase, opening it and grabbing the small black toolbox inside. I crack the lid, checking that it's all still there.

A blowtorch. A brand. Several knives of varying lengths. A length of piano wire. And overlooking all of it, a portrait of Aurelia was taped inside the lid, where she was blonde and beautiful and remote.

I smile at the picture and then close the lid, heading out of the room to get some answers about Birgit's death and The Brotherhood's involvement.

And if it so happened that there would be a little bloodshed? I wouldn't mind that at all.

GET A FREE BOOK!

Join my mailing list to be the first to know of new releases, free books, special prices and other author giveaways.

http://freehotcontemporary.com

ALSO BY JESSA JAMES

Bad Boy Billionaires

A Virgin for the Billionaire

Her Rockstar Billionaire

Her Secret Billionaire

A Bargain with the Billionaire

Billionaire Box Set 1-4

The Virgin Pact

The Teacher and the Virgin

His Virgin Nanny

His Dirty Virgin

The Virgin Pact Boxed Set

Club V

Unravel

Undone

Uncover

Club V - The Complete Boxed Set

Cowboy Romance

How To Love A Cowboy

How To Hold A Cowboy

Treasure: The Series

Capture

Control

Covet

Bad Behavior

Bad Reputation

Bad Behavior/Bad Reputation Duet

Beg Me

Valentine Ever After

Covet/Crave

Kiss Me Again

Contemporary Heat Boxed Set 1

Handy

Dr. Hottie

Hot as Hell

Contemporary Heat Boxed Set 2

Pretend I'm Yours

Rock Star

The Baby Mission

His Brother's Fiancee

ABOUT THE AUTHOR

Jessa James grew up on the East Coast but always suffered a severe case of wanderlust. She's lived in six states, had a variety of jobs and always comes back to her first true love – writing. Jessa works full time as a writer, eats too much dark chocolate, has an iced-coffee and Cheetos addiction, and can't get enough of sexy alpha males who know exactly what they want – and aren't afraid to say it. Dominant, alpha-male insta-luv is her favorite to read (and write).

Sign up HERE for Jessa's Newsletter:

http://jessajamesauthor.com/mailing-list/

BB

Lightning Source UK Ltd.
Milton Keynes UK
UKHW020645070922
408471UK00010B/1364

9 781795 923446